Falling for Trouble

The Dare to Fall Series
Book 1

NEW YORK TIMES BESTSELLING AUTHOR
Carly Phillips

Copyright © Karen Drogin 2026
Published by CP Publishing
Print Edition

Illustrated Cover Design: Concepts by Canea
Editing: Rumi Khan and
Claire Milto: BB Virtual Assistant for Authors

* * *

All rights reserved. No part of this book may be reproduced in any form by any means without the prior written consent of the Publisher, excepting brief quotes used in reviews.

This book is a work of fiction. Names, characters, places, and incidents either are products of the author's imagination or are used fictitiously. Any resemblance to actual events or locales or persons, living or dead, is entirely coincidental.

No part of this book may be used to create, feed, or refine artificial intelligence models, for any purpose, without written permission from the author.

This title claims exemption of the European Accessibility Act because the publisher qualifies as a micro-enterprise.

FALLING FOR TROUBLE

He's the bad boy my family warned me about— and the one man I can't have.

I just landed the job of my dreams—planning the Miami Thunder football team's anniversary celebration—and I can't afford distractions. Especially not tattooed billionaire and reformed troublemaker Lucas Carras. He exudes alpha-hero intensity, but he's been off limits for as long as I've known him.

But the kickoff party is happening at the nightclub he co-owns with my brother… and with my sibling out of town, I'm stuck working with Lucas.

Forced proximity ignites the desire we've both been pretending doesn't exist. From bedrooms to storage rooms, the scorching tension causes us to cross every line we swore we wouldn't. On paper, we're complete opposites. In reality, the chemistry is undeniable.

This party is everything I've worked for—my moment to prove myself. Until the sabotage starts.

Orders vanish. Vendors back out. Someone is determined to ruin the anniversary… and my reputation along with it.

Suddenly Lucas isn't just a distraction. He's my protector, my anchor, and the only man I trust to stand by my side.

But when my brother finds out about us, family drama explodes. And I'm torn between being the good girl who plays by the rules… and falling for trouble.

Acknowledgments

Drink recipes courtesy of Western US Speed Rack champion bartender Mak Kelly.

CHAPTER ONE

Rainey

IT'S PAST EIGHT p.m. and I stare at my phone, willing the damn thing to ring, but it remains silent.

Calm down, I tell myself.

Either Golden Palm Events, the company I co-own with my best friend, Kaylee Martin, will win the bid for the Miami Thunder football team's 50th anniversary celebration or we won't. But I need the stress of not knowing to end. We were assured an answer tonight, so we wait. Even Ashlynn, our receptionist, has gone home for the day.

"You do realize watching your phone won't make it ring faster?" Kaylee asks, as she sits at her desk, calmly drinking from her water bottle.

My stomach isn't just swirling in anticipation, it's rumbling with hunger, yet I'm too nervous to eat. "Winning this bid could put us on the map," I remind her. Not to mention give us badly needed positive press so we can finally put the past behind us.

My partner runs a hand through her blonde, high-lighted hair and tucks a few strands behind her ear.

"We're doing very well as it is. Do I want this job? More than anything, but it isn't worth the stress you're putting on yourself. Besides, did you forget your father owns the team?"

I shake my head because nepotism is the last reason I want this job. "That is exactly why I told him I want us to earn this opportunity on merit, or I don't want it at all. Besides, it's not just up to my dad, it's a group decision. And even if we legitimately get the opportunity to handle the Thunder's anniversary events, there are those who will scream preferential treatment anyway." I'll just have to work extra hard to prove myself.

Something I've been doing ever since being publicly accused of acting unprofessionally by a disappointed client who'd destroyed our reputation on social media and in the business circles where we want to work. In truth, the gentleman—and I use that term loosely—had been impossible to please and nothing I did for his event satisfied him.

Kaylee sighs. "People suck. Especially Gregory Atwater. But forget about the past. You must admit we nailed the Thunder presentation."

In front of my father, the general manager, the coach, and the head of PR, we gave a demonstration of our ideas for the season-long campaign. Even I can admit it was our best presentation to date. "We did an amazing job and no matter what happens, I'm proud of us."

"Me too," Kaylee says with a smile. "And don't worry about anyone claiming nepotism because we'll do such a great job, they'll forget your father is Ian Dare."

Unable to help myself, I snort. "Nobody will ever forget I'm Ian Dare's daughter." Don't get me wrong, I love both of my parents. My mom and I are super close, and I've always been a daddy's girl. Until it came to building my business.

Golden Palm Events is my pride and joy, and Kaylee and I have always been determined to make it in the corporate event planning world on our own and not thanks to my family name. The Dares are huge in football circles and not only because my father owns the team. My uncle Alex used to be the star quarterback for the Tampa Breakers, the Thunder's biggest rivals. Alex and my dad now work together on concussion protocol, CTE, and preparing young rookies for post-football life. Not to mention most of my family has worked or still works for the Thunder in some capacity. Every one of my relatives has offered to refer our business to their friends.

I politely refused. I'm lucky enough to have a trust fund that gave me the start-up money but everything else came from hard work and dedication, not family connections. Even after the initial social media hit that nearly destroyed us, we're accomplishing our goal. We already have a stellar list of clients, but there is no denying this party would put us at the top.

"Who else pitched?" Kaylee asks. "Do you know?"

I have inside connections and information thanks to Aunt Olivia and Uncle Dylan, who both work in the front office. I think about the names she gave me. "Angela Gunn pitched ideas, but she's a force in wedding and social party planning, not corporate events. Maybe she's looking to expand, but she doesn't have the résumé or the experience we do."

Kaylee nods. "I agree. I assume Blaire Reynolds put in a bid?"

I groan as I reply. "She did." Blaire owns what I can only call our biggest rival company.

No matter the opportunity, Sun Coast Events, Blaire's business, is always up against us. More often than not, we win based on our talent. I can only hope it's the same with the Thunder account.

I pace the room while Kaylee texts on her phone and the minutes drag by. Finally, I turn to her. "I'm going to the ladies' room. I'll be right—"

Before I can finish the sentence, the cell phone in my hand rings. I glance down to see my father's name and my stomach flips in anticipation.

I give Kaylee a nod. "This is it." We stare at each

other for a long second, then I tap the screen and put the phone to my ear. "Hello?"

"Hi, princess."

No matter how old I am, that's what my dad calls me. "Any news?" I ask him.

"Congratulations, you got the job!"

I love him for not hesitating before answering. "Oh my God, that's amazing! Thank you!" My heart pounds in my chest, excitement filling me as I grin at Kaylee, who pumps her fist in the air.

"You both earned it," Dad says, pride in his tone. "As promised, I sat back and let things happen. No push from me."

I purse my lips but remain silent. Knowing my father, he probably sang my praises, but I'm sure he didn't insist that my company win the bid. He respects my work ethic, and I know he'll honor my request. For the most part.

"Thanks so much! I have to go share the news with Kaylee, but we'll talk soon, okay?"

"Of course. Love you, and I'm proud of you," he says.

"Love you too!" I disconnect the call and let out an excited scream. "We did it!"

Kaylee rounds the desk and gives me a hug. Then we're jumping up and down like little kids who've been told they can go to the carnival.

"We should celebrate," Kaylee says. "We're going to be working hard this year, so let's take advantage of our downtime while we can. Let's have some fun."

I nod. "Want to go to Midnight?" I suggest my brother Jack's nightclub. He opened the club with his best friend, Lucas Carras, and another co-owner, Tristan Hayes, who'd inherited the building where the club, now a top luxury Miami night spot, is located.

"Yes. That's perfect." Kaylee's eyes gleam with anticipation. "I wouldn't mind a night staring at Tristan. The man is sex appeal personified."

I hold back a snicker. Though she has a thing for Tristan, I reserve that description for Lucas Carras, the dark-haired, Greek god who is my brother's bad boy best friend. The same man I've been warned away from since he was a troubled teen. But he's a grown man now with a solid business and thanks to his relationship with Jack, we have a friendship of sorts. Which doesn't mean I don't fantasize about him. Because I do.

"I'd love to go home and change before we go. Do you want to meet up outside the club?" Kaylee asks.

I nod. "I could use some fixing up myself." I don't want to show up at the club with my makeup smudged and my hair a mess from running my fingers through it. Not to mention, I'm wearing my professional outfit, a sleeveless camisole and a fitted pencil skirt ending above the knee, covered with a lace cardigan. Definitely not a nightclub look.

I text my brother and let him know we're coming by and to please reserve us a table. Then, Kaylee and I agree on a time to meet, and we each head home. In addition to showering, changing, and putting on makeup, I plan on eating some leftovers from last night so I don't drink on an empty stomach.

A little while later, on a high and feeling pretty damn good, I see Kaylee standing outside the club and I join her. Thanks to me being Jack's sister, we bypass the long line of people waiting to get in.

"Hi, James." I smile at the bouncer.

"Hey, Rainey. Go ahead," he says, gesturing for us to go inside.

Once in the club, low lighting surrounds us. Glass and chrome walls reflect the luxurious white leather seating, and the dance floor gleams with subtle up-lighting. I'm so proud of Jack and all he's accomplished with this place. My siblings and I all had the opportunity to work with the Thunder and made our decisions accordingly.

Jack and I are determined to make our own way while the twins work for the Thunder, under my dad. They're being groomed to take over, and they each bring different personality aspects to the job. Hudson and Miles are perfectly suited to lead the Thunder when the time comes. Meanwhile, my dad isn't going anywhere anytime soon. Retirement is not in the near future.

I walk past the dance floor, which is empty. The DJ doesn't start for another half hour, so people mill around, standing at tables and the bar, while a playlist booms from the speakers. As I head toward an empty space at the bar to order drinks, I'm feeling the music and I nod to the beat.

Once there, I turn to my friend. "What can I order for you?"

Kaylee pauses in thought. "A white Russian."

I grin, knowing how she loves anything sweet. I plan to order a glass of chardonnay for myself when I hear my name being called.

I turn to see my brother striding toward me, a bottle of champagne in one hand.

"Hey, you two! I hear congratulations are in order," Jack says, a smile on his face as he yanks me into an embrace. "Congrats, sis," his voice whispers in my ear.

"Thanks," I say, a lump rising in my throat. It's one thing to accomplish my goal, yet another to know my brother is genuinely happy for me.

Jack and I have always been close. I adore all three of my loving, *overprotective* male siblings. You'd never know I was the oldest the way they carry on, especially when I was younger. Nobody was good enough for me and they let any potential boyfriends know it. Even when the twins were young, they thought it was their job to protect me. Whispered instructions from my father, no doubt.

Releasing me, Jack turns to Kaylee. "Congrats to you, too. It's a huge get," he says.

Her grin matches mine. "Thanks, Jack." She pulls him into a sisterly hug. Kaylee and I have been friends since elementary school and Jack is like a brother to her, too.

"Now let's head to your table and celebrate," he says. "You two can order whatever you want on the house, but not before we toast your success."

He holds up the champagne and tips his head toward the private, elevated platform area reserved for Jack, Lucas, Tristan, and their guests. VIP patrons have separate private areas they can rent that overlook the lower floor of the club, but this is the owners' space.

I look up, surprised to see Tristan and Lucas already seated there. I thought it would just be us and Jack tonight.

"Oh!" Kaylee says, obviously pleased.

"The guys wanted to celebrate with you." Jack extends his arm, gesturing for us to walk ahead of him.

I step behind Kaylee and walk to the far staircase

that leads to the balcony. My gaze locks with Lucas and I trip. Jack grasps my elbow to steady me. My cheeks grow hot, and I look away. *Jeez, Rainey. Clumsy much?*

As we approach the table, both men stand. Tristan pulls me into a friendly hug. "Congratulations," he says, before stepping back and turning his attention to Kaylee.

Lucas steps up next. "I had no doubt you'd get the account." A sensual gleam lights his eyes, and his gruff voice turns me on. He doesn't even have to try. Sex appeal is just a part of who he is.

Though he can be withdrawn at times, as a club owner, he is also able to turn on the charm. And when he does? Ladies, watch out!

"Congratulations." He reaches out and I step into his arms.

Unlike Tristan, I feel this embrace all the way down to my toes. As I lean into him, my entire body tingles and when I draw a deep breath, I inhale his cologne. The masculine mix of smoke, citrus, and leather fills my nostrils, and I can't help but stay where I am for a second too long.

As usual, when I'm near Lucas, a longing to be more than friends fills me, but I know better. He has too many red flags to be an option for me, no matter how strong the attraction between us is. And I have no doubt that attraction is mutual; stares that last too long, brushes of our shoulders or hands that elicit sparks on my skin. But he's the ultimate playboy and I'm a relationship kind of girl. I've never seen him with a long-term girlfriend, and I've heard my brother talk. He doesn't do serious.

Add to that, he's Jack's best friend and partner, and given Lucas's reputation with women, I don't think my sibling would approve. I'd hate to come between my brother and someone so important to him, especially in business. Even if I was in the market for a relationship right now, Lucas isn't the right man for me.

I sigh and step out of his embrace. "Thanks," I say with a smile. "I appreciate you celebrating with us."

"Wouldn't miss it." He pulls out the chair next to him. "Have a seat," he says, and I slide in.

We're all sitting now and Jack gestures to a server who walks over. "What can I get you, Mr. Dare?"

"Sophie, can you bring us an ice bucket and open this for us?" He hands her the champagne bottle and settles in. "So, care to share your ideas for the Thunder's 50th?" he asks.

I glance at Kaylee who nods, indicating she wouldn't mind if we talked about it now. "I was going to set up an appointment with you to discuss things, but since you asked, part of our plan involves this club." I grin at my brother, and not because I'm looking for a favor. This proposal will put a lot of money in Midnight's coffers, but it never hurts to butter him up. "I was hoping we could set up a time to talk soon."

Before Jack can reply, Sophie returns with the ice, pops the champagne, and pours the bubbly into glasses which another server already set down in front of each of us.

She puts the bottle into the bucket. "Enjoy," she says, and walks away.

Jack raises his flute and everyone does the same, but it's Lucas who speaks first. "To the biggest and best corporate event company in Miami and its two fabulous owners." His gaze meets mine and I flush at the overstatement, but I'm secretly thrilled with his praise.

We all tap glasses before each taking a sip. The bubbles tickle my throat, and I moan at the taste. I've always been a champagne girl and this is top shelf.

I run my tongue over my lips. "Delicious." As I speak, my gaze strays to the man next to me to find him staring, his green eyes darkening, his stare focused on my lips.

Without breaking eye contact, he picks up his drink and takes a swallow of amber liquid from an old-fashioned glass. He's returned to his drink of choice after using the champagne to toast us, and that means something to me.

"Back to your question." Jack draws my attention away from Lucas. "I can't be your contact. I'll be away scouting a second location for Midnight for a week or so."

"That's so exciting! Where are you looking?" Kaylee asks.

"A few places," Tristan says. "Jacksonville, Nashville, and then Charleston, South Carolina."

Jack smirks. "We'll let you know once we narrow things down."

I roll my eyes. "Fine. Be secretive. But we can't wait until you get back to get started on the plans for the Thunder."

"Lucas can run point," my brother says. Since Tristan is more of a silent partner, I know he isn't an option.

"Oh. Okay, sure." My stomach flips at the idea of working with the man I'm so attracted to. It's not that I don't want to, I just know it's going to be difficult with the sexual attraction sparking between us.

"Okay with you?" Jack asks his partner.

Lucas, who is leaning back in his seat, glass in one hand, nods. "Of course."

His continuing stare leaves me lightheaded. "I'll call you to set up a time that's good for you," I manage to tell him.

"I'm looking forward to it." He finishes his drink and stands. "I have some things I need to handle. Congrats again, ladies."

"Thanks," Kaylee and I say at the same time.

I watch as he walks away, noting how well his shirt fits his muscular back, and wonder how I'm going to work side by side with this man and keep my sanity.

CHAPTER TWO

Lucas

IT'S A BITCH to want something you can't have. I ought to know. She's sitting in the VIP section. I nod at my manager and walk to the end of the bar, taking a seat and looking over my domain. That's what Midnight is. The dream I built from the ground up with my best friend, Jack, and Tristan, who we met our last year in college. When he inherited this building, the idea for Midnight was born.

After a shit ton of blood, sweat, and tears, we own the chicest, hottest nightclub in Miami, and there is no way I'm going to mess up the life I finally have by sleeping with my best friend and partner's sister. No matter how much I want to.

It would help if the attraction wasn't mutual, but I have no doubt it is. When I pulled her in for a congratulations hug, she lingered, her arms around my waist and her cheek pressed against my shirt. While I indulged in the feel of her enticing curves, she'd taken a long, deep inhale, remaining in my arms longer than necessary and leaving me with no doubt we were both fighting the same need.

Rainey is everything I like in a woman: petite with lush curves, breasts that would overflow my hands, and an ass I could hold on to while I fucked her hard and deep. Except not only is she Jack's sister, she's also a long-term relationship type of girl.

Being Jack's best friend means I have insight into her life: a high school boyfriend that lasted over a year, a college relationship during her junior and senior years, and aside from other men in her past, there was the dickwad she'd broken up with about a year ago. None of the Dares had liked her ex and when he'd asked Rainey to marry him, they all let out a sigh of relief when she said no.

It doesn't take a genius to see how different we are. I don't do relationships. I've seen how screwed up my family was and though my foster—now adoptive—parents have a loving relationship, my views have been skewed by sixteen years with a drug addict mother and a father who did everything to help and enable her. As a result, I don't get emotionally invested, preferring women who satisfy my needs but know the score. Another one of many reasons that puts Jack's sister off limits.

Though I must admit, if there is anyone who could tempt me to give a real relationship a shot, it's Rainey.

I glance at the dance floor, my gaze locking on the

subject of my desire, as she dances along with her friend and the crowd of people enjoying the techno beat. Wearing a royal blue, fitted dress that hits mid-thigh, she's a vision of luscious curves and beauty. Her chocolate brown hair hangs down her back in waves, long and tempting. A man could curl those locks around his hand and pull as he enters her from behind. My dick twitches at the thought, making me appreciate my black slacks and the dim lighting.

As the night wears on, drinks flow from the wait-staff and it's obvious from how she's dancing more freely that Rainey has passed her limit. She's celebrating and having fun, and I can't fault her for that, but I can watch and make sure no asshole tries to take advantage.

"Hey," Tristan says, joining me at the corner of the bar. "What's up?"

I glance at the man who helped make mine and Jack's dream possible. The three of us are a good team, each of us with our own responsibilities.

"Just keeping an eye on things," I tell him. On nights we're open, I always hang out on the floor.

Tristan raises his eyebrow. "Don't you mean keeping an eye on one person in particular?"

I stiffen, surprised I've given myself away. There's no doubt he's referring to Rainey, so I won't try and lie my way out, but the last thing I need is for Jack to realize I want his sister. "I'm just making sure the women are safe."

Tristan lets out a laugh. "If women aren't safe in our club, we have problem. But tell yourself whatever lets you sleep at night."

I ignore the ribbing.

He leans in, not just because it's hard to hear over the music, but I sense he has more to say that he doesn't want anyone to overhear. "Why the hell don't you make a move?" he asks.

I meet his gaze. "In what world would Jack think I'm good enough for his sister?"

"In what world are you not?" Tristan counters.

I'm not down on myself, never have been. I'm aware of how far I've come and I'm damn proud of it. That doesn't mean I can't accept reality. I've already listed in my head all the reasons Rainey and I can never be together, but a more important one exists and it's the one Tristan would understand the most.

Propping my arm on the counter, I meet his gaze. "The one where I have a record," I remind him.

"Expunged," he volleys right back. "You were sixteen and you've turned your life around since then."

My foster father was a judge. Thanks to his connections at the time, he made a deal. As long as I testified against the guys I ran with, and I was never arrested again, my record would be expunged at eighteen. Didn't mean I wasn't the person who was there when my friends planned a home invasion.

"Maybe so, but I remember the days when Jack's parents didn't approve of him hanging out with me." Not that they were wrong. "Turning my life around or not, I can't imagine Ian Dare would want me anywhere near his only daughter except as her brother's business partner. Besides, I don't want to fuck up our business by pissing off Jack. So, time to change the subject."

Tristan holds up his hands. "Fine. I get where you're coming from, but things change. So do people's opinions." He rises from his seat. "Jack left early but Mike and Layla are here, and they'll be closing," he says of our managers. "I need to head home, too. I have a meeting in the morning."

I nod. Tristan isn't just a club owner, he's a real estate mogul and his schedule isn't an easy one. Which is why he's our silent partner, though we get his input on anything important. "See you tomorrow night."

He nods once and walks off.

No sooner is he gone than my gaze darts back to the dance floor in time to see Rainey stumble into a man who grasps her forearms to steady her. I decide the women have had enough to drink and their fill of dancing, too.

I push back from my seat and make my way

through the crowd, knowing how to maneuver to get where I want to go and not get stuck behind groups who have no intention of stepping aside.

Rainey's hands are on the man's chest, and she tips her head back and laughs. "I've been such a klutz tonight!"

"Come on, let's keep dancing," Kaylee says, tugging her friend's arm.

"Yes! Let's!" Rainey spins away from the man I assume is a stranger and right into me. "Oops!" She tilts her head back and those gorgeous indigo eyes, an inherited family trait, stare into mine. "Lucas," she says in a breathless whisper.

"Time to go home, beautiful." The term of endearment slips out.

"But I'm having fun!"

My lips twitch but I don't want to encourage her, so I hold back a laugh. "And it's a good idea to leave while you still are." I hook my arm around her waist and when Kaylee turns, I grasp her arm. "Tell me you two didn't drive here," I say.

"We each took a rideshare," Kaylee replies.

They wouldn't be going home the same way. I don't want either tipsy woman alone with a stranger driving them. "I'll take you both home."

"You're such a good guy." Rainey leans into me. "I accept your offer. Right, Kaylee?"

"Ummm. Think Tristan wants to drive me home?" she asks on a giggle, and I realize she's more wasted than I thought. She'd never admit to those feelings sober.

"Let's go. I'm the only ride you two are going to get tonight."

Kaylee wobbles on her heels, following me off the dance floor and through the club while Rainey obediently clings to my arm. I stop by my office to lock it up, then lead the women out to my car.

"I'll take the back seat!" Kaylee says too loudly in my ear.

"I've got the front." Rainey releases my arm, and I manage to open the back door for Kaylee and then the front for Rainey.

I don't think either woman is at the going-to-puke stage, but I send up a prayer anyway.

I ask for their addresses and since Kaylee lives closer, I decide to take her home first. On the drive, both women are quiet. A glance in the rearview mirror and I see Kaylee asleep, her body leaning over and her head at an awkward angle.

To my right, Rainey is snoring lightly, her head tipped backward. I take in her lovely profile, her pert nose with freckles across the bridge, and the pouty lips I always find hard to resist. Also, as usual, I wonder what her mouth would taste like. Thank God I pull up to Kaylee's apartment building before a groan escapes the back of my throat.

I park the SUV and climb out. Once I walk Kaylee to the door, sign in with the doorman, and make certain she gets inside safely, I head back to deal with my final passenger.

I slide into my seat and shut the door.

"Hi," Rainey says from beside me. "I appreciate you driving us home."

"I didn't think either of you belonged in a rideshare with a stranger."

She nods. "I'm much more sober than I was. I'm sorry if you had to go out of your way."

I shake my head as I start the car. "I'm not, and even if I were, it's not a big deal."

"It is." She grows silent as I drive toward her apartment building and pull up in a circular driveway. After cutting the engine, I reach for my door handle. "You don't need to get out," she says.

"I'll walk you to your apartment." My tone brooks no argument.

Despite her saying she's sober, I've kept an eye on her for most of the night, and I don't want her tripping as she walks. Or maybe I'm not ready to say goodbye just yet.

She wrinkles her nose at me but finally lets out a sigh. "I know better than to argue with a determined man."

I chuckle. "I take it you have a lot of experience."

"Have you *met* my father and brothers?" she asks with a smile.

I step out of the vehicle and round the back, then hold the door open and extend a hand so she can more easily get out. I shut the door behind her and press the handle to lock the vehicle.

We walk toward the building and use the revolving door, stepping out into a white-and-gray marble lobby. I live a couple of buildings down the road, also on the ocean, and had no idea Rainey and I were within walking distance of each other. Given that we'll probably be working together, is it too close for comfort? Doesn't matter. I'm in it no matter what.

"Hi, Carl," Rainey says to the concierge. "Lucas is leaving his SUV out front. He's just going to walk me up to my apartment."

He nods. "No problem, Ms. Dare."

I place my hand on her lower back, and a subtle tremor runs through her at my touch. I clench my jaw and look straight ahead as she guides me toward the elevator. Though my palm presses against her dress, I swear I feel her body heat on my skin.

Once inside, she taps the PH button and steps away, placing her back against the wall so she's facing me. I'm not surprised she lives in the penthouse. She comes from old money and a father who would insist she has the best.

"I looked at this building before I bought my place," I tell her.

"Did you? I also checked out a couple of other apartment buildings, but this one was perfect. And it didn't need a ton of renovations, which is always a plus."

"I did have to renovate, but now my apartment suits me."

She smiles. "I'm glad."

The elevator comes to a stop and we step out. There are only two doors on the floor, one on either end of the hallway, and she turns right to her apartment.

Reaching into her purse she finds her keys. "So, I guess you can go now," she says as she puts her key in the lock.

"I could."

She turns back toward me, her head already tipped up so she can see my face. So petite and so fucking cute.

"Thanks again. For the ride," she says.

My gaze strays to her mouth. "My pleasure."

"Umm… mine too." Her eyes open wide. "I mean—"

I'm unable to hold back a laugh. "I know what you meant." Placing my hands on her shoulders, I turn her back toward her door before I do something stupid. Like dip my head and kiss those soft, pouty lips.

She turns the key, pushes open her door, and twists back around. "I'll call you to set up that appointment."

"Sounds good." And damn if I'm not looking forward to it.

She smiles, showing me her dimples. "And thank you again for the ride." Without warning, she lifts herself onto her tiptoes and kisses my cheek, giving me a brief hint of spicy cinnamon before she lowers herself to her feet.

Her cheeks are flushed red as she meets my gaze. "Night, Lucas."

I can't help but wink. "Night, Rainey."

CHAPTER THREE

Rainey

I WALK INTO the building where the front offices of the Thunder are located. Before I go to my father's, I stop by to see Hudson and Miles, but both are in meetings, so I head directly to my dad's office. The door is open and voices sound from inside.

"Dammit, Ian. Free up the funds we need for the CTE protocol I want to put in place," Uncle Alex says.

"If you'd let me finish a sentence, I'd tell you I already had." I hear the irritated tone in my dad's voice. Typical.

I hold back a snort of laughter. My father and uncle are close now, but I've heard stories about the early days when Dad met my mother and *she* was Uncle Alex's best friend. Mom going out with Dad pissed off my uncle because my father and Uncle Alex's family were estranged. My grandfather, Robert Dare, who nobody talks to or hears from, had a secret family—Alex's family—and the resentment on both sides was huge. My mother brought the families together, but my uncle and my dad still enjoy their bickering.

I knock on the open door. "Hello? Am I interrupting anything?" I look from man to man, Uncle Alex in a pair of jeans and a T-shirt, and my father in his usual suit and tie.

My dad's face softens when he sees me. "Come on in, princess."

"Rainey! It's good to see you." Uncle Alex steps forward and hugs me tight then releases me. "I hear congratulations are in order."

I grin. "They are and I'm excited about it, too." I turn to my father. "Actually, that's why I'm here. I was hoping we could talk about some things related to the anniversary." I glance back and forth between the two men. "Unless you two want to argue some more?"

Both let out a laugh.

"We're finished," says Uncle Alex. He presses a kiss to my head. "Take care."

"Give my love to Aunt Madison," I tell him.

"Will do. Talk to you later, Ian."

My father rolls his eyes as his half-brother leaves the room.

"Well, that was fun. Or, should I say, sadly normal?" I ask. "Do I need to tell Mom you've been giving Uncle Alex a hard time?" I know I'm stirring the pot, but I can't help it. It's too much fun.

He shakes his head. "You're trouble, do you know that?"

I merely grin.

"Your mother will always take my side," he says with the confidence of a man who is as in love with his wife now as he was the day he met her. To hear them tell the story, it was love at first sight. The minute Dad laid eyes on Mom, he knew she was it for him.

I sigh, wondering if I'll ever have a relationship like theirs. It's one to aspire to for sure.

"So, what brings you by?" he asks, and I'm grateful for the chance to get out of my own head. "And where's my hug?"

Grinning, I step around his side of the desk and hug my dad. Then I take a seat across from the desk and he settles in the chair next to me. "I wanted to go over the anniversary celebration. I thought we could kick off the season with a huge party at Midnight."

He nods thoughtfully. "I take it your brother approved."

I purse my lips, unsure how he'll like my answer. "Actually, Jack will be out of town, so I'll be working with Lucas. I have an appointment, but I've yet to run the idea by him fully."

He runs a hand over his face in silence. I know that's Dad's thinking expression.

"Are you sure a nightclub is the best venue for this?" he asks.

I nod. "Yes. I was there Saturday night and it's

perfect." I think back to that evening and despite being tipsy, I scouted the place thoroughly.

He smiles. "I have no doubt you checked it out."

I also got a little too close to Lucas, though I doubt my father would want to hear about that. Nor would he want to know I'd somehow, in my inebriated state, kissed Lucas on his cheek. The razor stubble brushed my lips and when I'd inhaled, he'd smelled delicious. Arousal washed over me and I'd had a hard time falling asleep, my thoughts consumed with him. Thanks to that kiss, as platonic as it was, I dread having to face him when we meet to discuss work. So much for being the complete professional, and though I want to groan, I do not want my father asking me what's wrong.

Taking my mind off Lucas isn't easy, but I refocus on the 50th anniversary plans. "Midnight has three floors and the rooftop, assuming it's a nice night. It's large, has the huge dance floor on the first level, bars on the others. Not to mention it benefits them if they agree. If we start the 50th celebration there, we can keep them involved throughout the season, have them sponsor some giveaways, and be part of the end-of-season celebration." There. That put me back on track.

"I'm sure Jack would agree. And Lucas, too. I'm just uncertain about the nightclub aspect," Dad says.

I rub my hands on my slacks, knowing I have

more in my arsenal to entice him. "See how you like this. By establishing a connection with a local business, we can tie the anniversary into the team's community outreach program. I know you and Uncle Alex are big on concussion protocol, and we can raise money for the high schools in the area while we celebrate the team this year."

He raises his eyebrows and a wide grin spreads across his handsome face. Even I know my dad is good-looking. It's been pointed out to me often enough. I take after him with the color of my eyes only. The rest of me, curves and hair color, is all Mom. And I have no complaints at all.

"I think it's a fabulous idea, my brilliant daughter." He leans in closer to me. "Now, tell me why you look like you're exhausted and haven't slept." His hand brushes across my cheek.

And there's the overprotective dad I know and love. "I'm fine. I was out late Friday night and worked all weekend on the details of the Thunder anniversary, that's all."

He narrows his gaze. "Fine. But get some sleep," he orders.

I don't roll my eyes. I'd never be outright disrespectful to Dad. "I'll try," I say.

"Good enough."

"I have to get to the office," I tell him.

He rises to his feet and I do the same. "Now give your old man another hug and promise you'll come home for dinner soon."

I smile. "That, I can do. Bye, Dad." I leave on a high, feeling proud of myself. I've never found it difficult to make my parents proud, but this time? Knowing it's been hard-earned? I'm floating.

I stop by a drive-through Starbucks on my way back to my office, picking up an iced venti chai latte for me, a regular latte for Ashlynn, and Kaylee's favorite flavored drink. By the time I arrive at the office, it's almost ten but I've already let them know I'll be in late.

I push open the door and walk into my office, pausing by Ashlynn's desk. "Hi, Ashlynn. How are you?" I ask. "I got you a regular latte." I place the cup on her desk.

She slides her dark hair off her shoulders and smiles. "Thank you! That's so sweet. And I'm good, thanks. You?"

"I'm great," I tell her.

She grins. "Kaylee told me the good news. Congratulations."

I nod. "Thank you." I keep walking and join Kaylee in our shared office space. "An iced venti caramel latte for you," I say, handing her the large cup.

"I love you! I've been dragging since I woke up on

Saturday." She flops back in her chair.

Laughing, I lower myself into the seat behind my desk. "Tell me about it. My father called me out for looking tired. No wonder I rarely drink more than one glass of alcohol anymore."

"Ah, the perks of getting older," she says.

"Bite your tongue. We're not ancient." I shudder at the thought, though the idea of turning thirty is a gut punch.

"How did the meeting with your dad go?" Kaylee asks.

I grin. "He loves the idea of coordinating with Midnight. I had to throw in community outreach, but that's only going to make this idea better."

She takes a sip of her latte. "So, what's next?"

"The meeting with Lucas is next. That will get the ball rolling."

She props her chin on her hands and grins. "I'd like to be a fly on the wall for that meeting."

Shaking my head and not wanting to get into my feelings for Lucas, I glance down and start to sort through the mail sitting on my desk. These days, most things come via email but there's always something that shows up the old-fashioned way, so I make sure to check it all.

As I flip through, a familiar-looking picture catches my attention. "A postcard with a Thunder stadium logo." I wrinkle my nose. Last time I saw one of these was at a merch shop at the stadium. "Why would someone send this to me?" I turn it over to see a note in red marker on the back.

You think you're special but you're not. You don't deserve good things. Go away!

"What the hell is this?" I ask, a shiver going through me.

Kaylee rises from her seat, rounds her desk, and comes up behind me. "Oh my God!" She rips the postcard from my hand. "Who would send something like this?"

I spin my chair around so I can see and talk to her. She looks at both sides of the card, her eyes narrowing.

"What's wrong?" I ask.

"Look. There's no stamp on this. Ashlynn!" she calls out to our receptionist.

The pretty brunette rushes into the room. "What's wrong?"

"Did you bring in the mail?" I ask, pointing to the pile on my desk.

Her eyes open wide. "Ye-yes. Why?"

Kaylee waves the postcard at her. "Was this in there?"

Ashlynn shrugs her shoulders. "I don't know. I

didn't look through it. I just left it for Rainey with the other mail."

"Okay, thank you, Ashlynn. You can go back to your desk." I'm not sure why, but I want to keep this between myself and Kaylee.

Once the tapping of her heels stops, Kaylee tosses the postcard onto my desk. "I don't like this."

Kaylee is a huge true crime fan and I don't need her going off the rails on this. "It's creepy, but I doubt it's anything to worry about."

She frowns. "I suppose you're right. What about calling the police?"

"Because of a freaky postcard that's vaguely threatening? They have better things to do. Besides, without a postmark they'll have nothing to go on."

She sighs heavily. "Fine. You're right. It's probably just a sick joke."

I can't say I like someone who knows where I work dropping off a targeted postcard, but that's all it is. A piece of paper.

"Maybe you should tell one of your brothers?" Kaylee suggests. "I mean, I once saw a true crime show and the girl who was murdered was getting anonymous letters first."

"Kaylee!" I rub my hands over the goosebumps on my arms. "You're freaking me out. Just stop."

My friend glances down. "Sorry. I tend to get carried away."

"I know, and it's fine. But I am not telling my brothers, and neither are you. They'll tell my parents and my dad will flip out. And then he'll get overprotective and I'll have no peace. So promise me."

She nods and holds up one hand. "I swear."

I breathe a sigh of relief. Something makes me toss the postcard in a drawer instead of in the trash, and then I put it out of my head and get to work.

CHAPTER FOUR

Lucas

A WEEK AFTER I last saw Rainey at the club, I approach the front of the warehouse where her office is located. She's on the first floor in a private loft space. I open the door and a young brunette sits at a desk facing the street.

"Hi, can I help you?" she asks, looking up from her phone.

From what I can tell, she's not working all that hard. Then again, maybe she just answers the phone. I nod. "I'm here to see Rainey."

She nods. "I'll let her know you're here."

"No need." Rainey steps up behind her, and I'm blown away by how beautiful she looks in a pair of black slacks, black high heels, and a fitted blouse that shows off her curves. That beautiful brown hair is pulled into a ponytail with strands falling around her face with barely a hint of makeup. She doesn't need it—she's stunning. And I know working together and keeping my hands to myself won't be easy.

"Ashlynn, why don't you take an early lunch? Mr.

Carras and I have things to discuss."

"If you're sure," she says, and Rainey nods. Ashlynn rises from her seat. "Great! I have some errands to run before I grab something to eat."

Rainey smiles. "Take your time. Kaylee is out meeting with a client, and I don't need any help here."

Ashlynn takes her bag and slings it over her shoulder. "I'll be back later. Bye!" She walks out, leaving us alone, which won't help with my restraint, either.

"Well, welcome to Golden Palm Events," Rainey says with a sweep of her arm. "Come on back."

I head behind Ashlynn's desk and come up beside Rainey. Unable to help myself, I lean down and brush a kiss over her soft cheek.

She blinks in surprise, but I don't miss the shudder that ripples through her body. "What was that for?" she asks.

I grin. "A hello. I wanted to, and now we're even." For the light touch of her lips that I haven't been able to get out of my mind since last week.

Blushing and speechless, she tips her head toward the inner office area. "Come in and I'll show you around. This is the office." She gestures to two desks across from one another. "Kaylee and I wanted to be close so we can talk through ideas," she explains.

The shared space is modern with light cream hardwood floors, and a combination of plum and the same cream paint on the walls. Matching area rugs are strategically placed on the floor and facing us behind the desks are partition doors hiding what's behind them.

Rainey steps over and slides one side open. I follow her into a designer's dream of pinboards containing ideas, photos, fabrics and more, surrounded by walls and windows.

I can't help but be impressed with the business she and Kaylee have built. "This place is amazing."

She turns to me, smiling. "I love it. I really wanted a loft with open space and when I found this available for rent, I knew it was perfect." She gestures for me to follow, and we walk to a table by a window set with water bottles and what looks like fresh muffins. "I thought we could sit here and discuss my concepts and see if you're interested in partnering Midnight with the Thunder's 50th anniversary season."

"And you're buttering me up with food?" I ask, picking up a muffin and taking a bite. Blueberry sweetness explodes on my tongue.

She laughs and the sound echoes in the room. "I hadn't thought about it that way, but if it works, it works."

"Let's say you're off to a good start." I pull out a chair and sweep my arm, indicating she should sit.

"Thank you," she murmurs, lowering herself into

the seat. "I appreciate it. Not all men are that polite."

I raise a shoulder, though she can't see. "I didn't grow up with parents who taught me manners—" Yelling at each other was more like it. "But my adopted family did." Now why had I admitted even that much about my past?

I already know what her parents thought of me way back when Jack became my friend. Though I don't know if their opinion has changed in the years since, I don't care. I know my own worth. Another lesson courtesy of the Carras family and one I was happy to learn.

"I'm glad they were there for you when you needed them," she says, without questioning me more about my past.

I nod. "They're good people."

"Jack really likes them," she murmurs.

I sit beside her. "So, where do we begin?" I ask, eager to change the subject.

"Okay, our proposal to the Thunder involves a huge pre-season party for the team, their significant others, front office staff, and the like. I'd love to have that at Midnight, and before you say no because you'd have to close up for a night, I have permission to make it worth your while."

"You've piqued my interest. Go on."

After Rainey mentioned wanting to meet with us,

my partners and I already discussed the possibility of teaming up with the Thunder and agreed it will be a win-win for both businesses. The details will need to be hammered out, and I need to hear more of what Rainey has to say, but I'm going into this meeting with an open mind.

She continues her pitch, describing the connection she thinks Midnight and Golden Palm Events can make with combined charity outreach. We discuss celebrating the history of the team and the legendary coaches and players who have come before. She's already spoken to the PR people in the front office about creating a highlight reel to be shown during halftime of the first game, and she suggests that Midnight open a concession booth featuring specialty cocktails geared toward the team's name.

"And the pièce de résistance? I have a meeting with the curator of a local museum to discuss a temporary historical exhibit to display team memorabilia, such as photographs, old uniforms, and trophies. It's going to be bigger than just one or two anniversary events." She sounds as proud of herself as she should be as she winds up her pitch. "And I realize some of this doesn't involve Midnight, but what do you think of the parts that do?"

She looks to me for my approval and my answer. I'm damn impressed and interested. "Fantastic ideas,"

I tell her. "Midnight is in." I reach out a hand.

She immediately places her palm against mine and curls her fingers around my hand. "Deal," she says with a huge smile.

I, meanwhile, am having a hard time focusing on anything but the soft feel of her skin and the scent of warm amber that clings to the air around me.

"I'm so excited!" She pulls her hand back and rubs it against her slacks, looking everywhere but at me. At least I'm not the only one affected by our close proximity. "I know we're going to make a great team. There's just one more thing."

"And that is?" I ask.

"Kaylee is busy with another account, and I was hoping you would help me out with the Thunder events. The cross promotion will help Midnight, too. I have a staff when it comes to setup and takedown, but there may be things I need a hand with."

What she's asking means we'll be spending more time together, something I'm all for. I'm just surprised she wants to do the same, but I'm not going to argue. "Jack's away but Tristan is around for any emergencies at the club. If you need my help, just ask."

"Perfect. I have such a good feeling about this. Thank you, Lucas."

"My pleasure. I'll talk to Mak, our best bartender, and ask her to come up with themed drinks. Once she's ready, you can come to the club, try them out, and give your thumbs-up… or -down." I laugh, and so does Rainey.

I glance at my watch and groan. "I need to get back to the club for a meeting with a vendor." My time with Rainey has gone on longer than expected, but I don't mind. I enjoy seeing her in her element, doing what she does best. I rise from my seat.

Rainey stands. "I'll walk you out." She escorts me through the back room, then the office until we reach the front door. "Thanks again for coming and listening to my plans."

I nod. "I'll be in touch soon for the drink tasting."

I'll only admit it to myself, but I can't wait to see her again.

CHAPTER FIVE

Rainey

As I DRIVE to Midnight, my thoughts are consumed with Lucas. It's been almost a week since our meeting about the Thunder project, and I can't stop thinking about him. How seamlessly we talked through my concepts and his approval of them all. I love my brother but if I'd met with him and not Lucas, he'd have had his own take on things and we'd have ended up butting heads. Typical siblings. Instead, I'd been able to float on a high as I began to make phone calls and talk to vendors for many of my ideas. Jack's excitement when I'd gotten the job had felt great, but Lucas's approval was next level.

I'd also gotten a small glimpse into his past, how his biological parents hadn't taught him manners. It was a small thing but a big admission. Given what I know of his childhood, growing up in a rough downtown area and hanging with the wrong crowd, I have a feeling them *not* teaching him manners was better than the things they *had* done. Those details my parents kept from me, and I've never had a reason to ask.

Now, if I learn them at all, I want it to be from Lucas.

It's midday Thursday and the club is closed to guests. As I walk inside for the drink tasting, butterflies take flight in my stomach. I'm excited to see what Mak, the bartender and mixologist who's been with Midnight since they opened, has created. But I'm anticipating seeing Lucas even more.

"Hello!" I call out, and a blonde head pops up from behind the counter.

"Rainey, hey!" Mak glances at her watch. "Right on time."

"Punctual as ever." I roll my eyes in a self-deprecating acknowledgment of my personality. I've inherited that trait from my dad. Not all my siblings have it and it's one that serves me well in business.

Doing my best not to look around for Lucas like a lovesick teen, I slide onto a stool, ready to get to work, though drink tasting is the fun part of the job.

"Let me ping the boss," Mak says, reaching for her phone. "We can't get started without him."

My stomach flips again, and I settle in to wait. It isn't long before I hear footsteps and I turn to see Lucas walking across the floor in long strides. Dressed in his typical collared shirt, unbuttoned just enough to catch a sprinkling of dark chest hair on his tanned skin, I have the sudden urge to grab the edges of that shirt and rip them open so I can see the muscles beneath. It doesn't help that as he gets close, I see the edges of a black tattoo peeking through.

Holy hell, this man is hot.

His eyes lock on mine. "Welcome to Midnight," he says with a sweep of his arm, and I know he's mimicking my greeting when he'd come to my office. He's not mocking me, he's grinning and winks as I laugh.

"The floor is yours," Lucas tells Mak, sliding onto a barstool beside me.

"Okay, let's get this party started!" the pretty bartender says. She reaches below the counter and suddenly music surrounds us. Not too loud like a normal night, but just enough to give us ambiance.

"I waited for you so I could make each drink fresh," she says, taking out three drink glasses.

An idea strikes me, and I decide I'm going to order engraved glasses with the Thunder logo and *50th Anniversary* etched on them.

"I'm going to make all three and leave you to taste at your leisure," Mak tells me. "And if you don't like one, I can come up with something new."

"Thanks! I can't wait to taste your creations."

Mak gets to work and Lucas leans close, one elbow on the bar. "So, how was the rest of your week?"

"Busy as usual. Yours?" Because I'm much more interested in what he has to say than my week of phone calls and appointments, forced smiles when I didn't like ideas, and real ones when the vendors were easy to work with.

He shrugs. "The same as yours. Busy. Your brother enjoys the hands-on part of the business, and I prefer… watching over the business. But with Jack out of town, I'm dealing with *people*." He shudders, making me laugh.

"Who knew you weren't a people person?" I ask.

He sobers a bit, and his shoulders stiffen, his easygoing manner turning to a more withdrawn one. "I used to be a people person. Hung out with a big group of guys."

"And you don't anymore?" It's my turn to prop an elbow on the bar and lean close. I didn't expect to learn about him today, and I'm all in.

He shakes his head. "I discovered that big groups can lead to bigger problems."

"I see…" I don't, but I want to. "What happened?" I ask.

"So let me tell you about the first drink," Mak says, interrupting whatever I might have learned about Lucas, but I tuck away the information to ask again at a more appropriate time. "I named it The Touchdown."

"I like it already," I tell her, excited to taste.

She laughs. "What makes this drink special is also what takes the longest to prepare. I toasted black sesame seeds ahead of time. You do them over medium heat until they're fragrant and begin to pop." She brings a container from beneath the bar to show me. "Then, while they're cooling, I combined equal parts Jamaican rum and a rye blend, leaving some space for the seeds. Seal it and shake well. Then leave it for three to five days so it infuses."

My eyes are wide as I listen to the preparation that's gone into the drink. "Thanks for explaining. I've never thought about what goes into mixing drinks, but I admit to being fascinated… and impressed."

"Mak here is a Western US Speed Rack Champion. It's an all-female high speed bartending competition," Lucas says, pride in his tone. "We're lucky to have her working for us."

Mak waves off the compliment. "What's most important is that the competition raises money for breast cancer charities. But winning is awesome too." She laughs. "Now, as for the drink, I combine the ingredients in a mixing glass, including the seeds." As she pours, she names each ingredient: banana liquor, demerara gum syrup, orange bitters, a pinch of salt, and lemon and orange expression. "Add ice," she says, as she does just that, continuing to explain the process while she works. "Stir until chilled and diluted, strain over fresh ice in a rocks glass, and garnish with lemon and orange peels." She adds the topping. "Here you go!" She pushes the dark brown drink toward me.

Picking up the lowball glass, I take a sip and the nutty yet tropical taste explodes on my tongue. It's a bit sweet along with the depth of the rum. Delicious. "Your talent is incredible to watch and taste," I tell her. "This is perfect for a signature drink!"

"I know," she says with a grin.

"She's modest, too." Lucas laughs.

I take another sip. "I could finish this whole glass, but I know we have two more drinks to go, and I don't want to drink and drive."

Lucas leans in close once more, the warmth of his body and spicy scent of his aftershave a reminder of all the ways I'm attracted to him. It takes all my restraint not to lean back against his broad chest.

"I've always got you," he says in a gruff, rumbly voice. "But in this case, I think you're right. Let's move on to drink number two." He straightens his posture and I miss his closeness.

He strides around the bar, joining Mak on the other side.

"Okay, next up is the Sports Star Martini," she says.

"Nice name," Lucas says.

I nod in agreement.

Mak pours water from a tap and slides a glass to me. "Take a couple of sips to clear your palate."

I do as instructed and wait eagerly for her next creation.

Again, she explains as she prepares the drink, the same way she did for The Touchdown, then slides what she calls a coupe glass toward me. "Give it a try."

I lift it by the top, careful with the long stem. From the bright yellow color, I know there's going to be a citrus flavor. Sure enough, I taste a tangy, juicy yet bubbly drink, picking up the hint of vanilla and ginger spice, which I know from her description.

"Yum. Our guests will have a difficult time choosing, that's for sure." I run my tongue over my top lip, enjoying the hint of orange, and I moan at the flavorful, zesty tang.

My gaze lands on Lucas, only to find his eyes dark and his stare locked on my mouth. Warmth rises to my cheeks at the heat in his gaze, and between my thighs, a tingle of arousal reminds me there's nothing simple about being around him.

"Don't forget there's one more drink, with what I think is the best name. Thunder and Lightning." She sweeps her arm with a flourish and I'm grateful for the interruption.

I clap, because her specialty drinks have exceeded any expectations I had or hoped for. With each thing I nail down, my optimism for the Thunder anniversary grows stronger.

Mak repeats her presentation as she mixes the last drink, a yellowish green margarita. I'm fascinated as she floats what she says is a layer of high proof alcohol on top, lights it with a long lighter, then quickly extinguishes the flame with a mug over the top. It's a show stopper, for sure.

I take a sip and find it's ultra spicy with a hint of decadent chocolate. In fact, it might be my favorite. I meet Mak's gaze.

"Well?" she asks.

"Perfection. Honestly, I'm blown away."

"You like all three? No changes?" she asks.

I shake my head. "Nope. Not that I'd know how or what to suggest if I did want something different. But I love them all. Thank you!"

She bows at my words. "Then my job here is done. I'll leave you two to discuss and come back to clean up later. I need to do inventory in the storage room."

"Thanks, Mak," Lucas and I say at the same time.

She waves and heads toward the back of the club.

"Are you sure you're happy? I wouldn't want you to settle just to be nice," Lucas says.

"The drinks are perfect. *She's* perfect. You're right. Midnight is lucky to have her."

He returns to my side of the bar. "When we opened the bar, I went on a search for an ultra-talented bartender. She was between gigs and happy to move to Miami."

"Well—" Before I can finish the sentence, Lucas's cell phone rings. He looks down and furrows his brow. "Excuse me. I need to take this."

He takes a few steps away, and I watch him as he talks on the phone. His shoulders straighten, his muscles stiffen, and he runs his hand through his hair in frustration. He seems to listen more than talk, then disconnects the call.

I quickly glance at my phone and open an app so I look like I've been busy and not staring or trying to eavesdrop.

"I'm back," he says.

I place my phone on the bar and lift my head to meet his gaze. Instead of the easygoing guy discussing drinks, a moodiness seems to have settled around him. His eyes appear hooded, his aura much darker than when we'd been playfully discussing drinks.

"Is everything okay?" I ask.

"Yeah." He eases back onto the stool beside me and silence takes over. Instead of talking, I wait for him to decide if he wants to confide in me.

"Remember what we were talking about before?" He drums his fingers on the bar.

I tip my head to one side. "Can you be more specific?"

"About hanging out in large crowds not being a

great thing?" He stands up and walks back around the bar until he's behind it.

Grabbing a glass, he pours himself what looks like bourbon, then takes a large sip, and suddenly, I'm hit by the apparent gravity of whatever he's about to tell me.

"I remember. What about it?" I ask, wanting to encourage him to open up.

He braces his hands on the counter in front of him. "When I was young and before the Carrases adopted me, my parents were useless. Mom was a drug addict and Dad an enabler. I was just an annoyance to them both. Always in the way. She needed whatever money Dad earned for her next fix and Dad was… mentally absent. The cabinets were often empty because she forgot to buy food and he spent his time down at the local bar."

I can't imagine the childhood he's describing. Coming from a large family of people who cared, who were always in each other's business, with parents who made sure we were safe, his description leaves me hollow inside, and that was just a bare-bones accounting of what he experienced.

I'm sure the little details were worse, but I hear the pain in his voice, and it resonates deep inside me. "I'm listening," I say softly.

He draws a steadying breath. "I didn't live in a

great neighborhood and the kids I hung with weren't good ones."

When he dips his head, I know he's ashamed of what he's about to tell me, so I sit quietly and wait.

"It started with petty burglaries. I was only sixteen, so I'd drive while others went inside. Then, one night, I drove as they did a *job*, they called it. A home invasion in an upscale neighborhood, and they'd gotten out with expensive items to sell. They'd also been caught by the homeowner's father, an older man they'd cold-cocked so they could escape."

I stifle a gasp. "You were with them?" I can't fathom Lucas being part of something violent.

He shakes his head. "In the car, which as you probably know, still makes me an accomplice." He doesn't meet my gaze. "It turned my stomach, and I couldn't live with what had happened. I figure it was Jacinda and Matthew's influence," he says, speaking with warmth along with regret in his voice. "So, I told Matthew."

"Your foster father."

"Yes," he says, and I'm happy to see him glance up and the light back in his eyes. The Carrases had adopted him, giving him the home and the true family he'd never had.

"What did he say?" I ask, leaning toward him, invested in the story. In Lucas.

He rubs his hands together and hesitates, obviously gathering his thoughts. "He insisted I go to the police and tell them what happened."

"That couldn't have been easy." Not for a sixteen-year-old boy with loyalty, I think to myself.

"It wasn't. It meant snitching, but I did it and they were arrested." He draws another deep breath. "I had to testify against my friends."

I shake my head at the situation he found himself in. "But were they *really* your friends?"

"No," he admits. "But where I come from, you didn't tell on *anyone*. Snitching was worse than any other crime I could have committed," he explains.

"What happened?" I ask.

He lifts the glass to his lips and takes a hefty drink. "Well, Richie was fifteen and given community service to teach him a lesson. The driver, Benny, got six months. But the oldest, Trick, is Benny's brother. He was the one who'd knocked out the old man. He was twenty-one, an adult, and had priors. Added to that, they found a gun stashed in his car and another in his pocket when they picked him up. He went away for a long while."

I let out a whistle. "It sounds like he deserved the time he served."

Lucas nods. "He did. And that phone call I just got was the Bureau of Prisons letting me know Trick is out."

"Oh no. I'm sorry." I wonder if there's danger involved in the man's release, but something keeps me from asking.

"With a little luck, I won't run into him," he mutters, and takes a sip, finishing off his drink. "Okay, so get back to Mak's cocktails. You're settled on all three?"

Taking the hint to change the subject, I refocus on the Thunder party. "I am. It's like I said, I love them. Mak came up with great ideas and they taste delicious."

"Perfect."

An awkward silence settles between us, and I understand. He'd opened up to me and been vulnerable, and now? He probably needs to regain his equilibrium. If I'm feeling off-kilter after what I'd learned about his past, he must be experiencing the same emotions, not to mention being shaken up by the call.

The fun mood from earlier is long gone, and I sense it's my time to leave.

I rise from my seat. "I should let you get back to work." Or to his thoughts.

He nods. "Come on. I'll walk you to your car."

"You really don't need to." It doesn't take a genius to know he wants time to process things, but his penetrating stare tells me he's not giving me a choice.

"Okay, sure." We make our way through the club.

"Will you thank Mak again for me? I'm excited about her drinks. In fact, I'm going to do themed glasses with the Thunder logo and a 50th anniversary graphic."

"Love that idea," he says, then pushes open the door, and I step out.

My car is in the first spot out front, and we stop by the driver's side door. Before I open it, I turn toward him. "I appreciate today, thanks." I use my key fob to unlock the car.

"You're welcome." He opens the door for me and pauses. "Rainey, wait."

"Yes?"

He scrubs a hand over his handsome face. "I thought I wanted to be alone, but… do you want to get lunch?"

I nod before I can think it through and once I have? I'm still going to say yes. I know I'm asking for trouble, but I can't bring myself to care.

"What did you have in mind?"

He treats me to a sexy grin, his good mood seemingly back. "It's a surprise, so you'll just have to wait and see."

CHAPTER SIX

Lucas

I NEARLY LET the news about Trick ruin my day, until I see Rainey about to get into her car. Suddenly letting her drive off didn't seem like a good idea. Though I'm hungry, I'm not in the mood for a sit-down restaurant.

I hope she's adventurous because I'm not taking her for a typical date. Not that this is a date. Which is a good thing because the place I have in mind isn't the elegant type of eatery a woman like Rainey deserves. It's my favorite take-out joint and serves as a reminder of our differences.

Although I have an SUV, today's beautiful weather means I drove my convertible to work. We take my vehicle with the promise I'll bring her back to the club later to pick up her car.

As I drive, I think back to our conversation, still surprised I spilled my guts, something I don't normally do. My business partners know my history because Jack was around back then, and I wouldn't go into business with either man without being one hundred percent honest. Beyond that, I never talk about those days.

But Rainey was there when the call came in and she'd been a good listener. I'd felt comfortable confiding in her even if the admission hadn't been easy. In fact, it had been mortifying admitting details of how I'd grown up and the things I'd done. Instead of being horrified, Rainey had been understanding and accepting, making me feel okay about my past and the things that were out of my control.

I pull into a parking spot by a food truck on the beach and turn to my passenger. "Here we are."

She lifts her sunglasses so I can see her gorgeous eyes. "A food truck? Really?" She unhooks her seat belt and is reaching for the handle before I can get out of the car to help.

I wondered how she'd feel about such a casual meal, and I have my answer. The more I learn about her, the more I realize she's everything I would want in a woman, assuming I was looking. But I'm not, no matter how perfect Rainey seems.

As I walk around the back of the car, I count all the reasons we can only be business colleagues, or, at the very most, friends. And when my phone in my pocket rings, and I pull it out to see her brother's name, my reasons are reinforced. I send the call to voicemail and decide to just enjoy Rainey's company for the afternoon.

We wait in line to order, and she chooses an over-stuffed roast beef sandwich with a huge variety of toppings, a tub of French fries, and a large soda.

"A girl after my own heart," I say as she accepts the sandwich from the server inside the truck.

"What do you mean?" she asks, as she takes a fry and pops it into her mouth.

I watch as her pink-colored lips move as she finishes and swallows the fry, doing my best not to think about her glistening mouth and the things I'd love to do to it and to her. Nothing she needs to know. As I glance down, it's pretty damn obvious what I'm thinking.

I shift toward the truck, waiting for my food as I answer her. "I like that you ordered a full sandwich and not a salad. That you're willing to eat around me and not starve yourself. I've seen too many stick-thin females, and frankly, it's not appealing."

The server calls out a number, and I move to the window to pick up my order. It's late for lunch, so Rainey and I are able to snag an empty picnic table that overlooks the beach and sit across from each other.

"I'm going to be honest," she tells me. "I take after my mom, so I'm never going to be *stick-thin*," she says, using air quotes around the words.

I think her curves are perfect, but I'm aware it's

inappropriate to say so. "You're perfect just the way you are." *Shit.*

"Well, thank you." Her cheeks flush, made more visible by the sun shining down on us. She swipes at her hair, then clears her throat, obviously and adorably flustered. "I enjoy my carbs and sugar too much to give them up. And I work out just enough to alleviate any guilt for eating what I love. But not too often." As if to prove her point, she picks up the huge sandwich and takes a big bite.

Grinning, I do the same with mine.

We eat in comfortable silence until she finally groans and pushes her paper plate away. "I am *full.*" She places her hand on her stomach. "And despite what I said, I *will* hit the gym after this because I feel overfed." She laughs out loud, a sound that goes straight to my cock.

"I go to the gym nearly every day," I tell her.

She raises her eyebrows. "Really?" She looks me over, her eyes darkening. "It shows, even though you're dressed."

"Sounds like it's my turn to say thank you," I say.

Her blush gets redder. "Do you like the gym? Because I despise it," she admits.

"I do." I run a hand over my face, realizing it's about to be more revelation time. "After *it* happened—"

"What you told me about earlier?" Her voice is low and soft.

"Yeah. That incident was the final straw after a bunch of smaller incidents. After I came to live with Jacinda and Matthew, I was a little shit, causing problems in school, getting into fights. I didn't hang out with those guys because they were my friends. They had issues, too. Like me." My hand goes to the skin above my heart, the skull tattoo on my left pec that bears evidence of those days. Dark times and darker themes, I think to myself.

"I know you went through a hard time, but you should be proud of where you are now," Rainey says.

I raise an eyebrow. "You *know*? Or you assume?" I ask because I'm well aware her parents didn't want Jack to be friends with me. Plus, Jack knows a shit ton more about my past than I normally reveal to anyone. I never thought about him repeating it to anyone, especially his sister, and I stiffen at the possibility of him sharing my darkest days.

"I... I know Jack and my parents used to argue about the time he spent with you. And back then, they warned me to stay away from you. But that was the past. They're proud of what you, Jack, and Tristan have built," she rushes to say.

I doubt her parents are proud of *me*, but I appreciate her trying to save her mother and father with the admission.

I merely nod. I need to change the subject and think back to what we'd been talking about when things felt lighter. "Well, once that night happened, Matthew taught me to redirect the anger and frustration I carried about my past, my present, and anything that was bothering me into working out."

Her gaze softens. "I like that for you. I'm sure it helped."

I think back to the first time my fist struck the punching bag, how those blows freed me from the buzzing anger that had always been with me. Especially after I'd learned how my parents died. "Boxing helped a lot. I liked getting stronger, feeling more in control." And that's why I keep it up to this day.

"Makes sense to me. And Lucas?" she asks, as she gathers our plates. "You shouldn't be embarrassed about where you came from. It formed the man you are today." She rises from the bench without meeting my gaze. "Besides, bad boys have a certain appeal." Without another word, she strides to the already overflowing garbage pail and pushes our plates inside.

No doubt she rushed off because she didn't want me to catch her blushing, but all I can think of is her admission that tells me this attraction isn't one sided. Not at all.

We walk to my car in charged silence. The warmth

from the sun beats down on our heads, but I grew up in Florida, as did Rainey. We're used to the heat and humidity.

I open her door and she slides in. It's not my fault if my stare lands on her tanned legs beneath her skirt, and my cock gives another jolt of awareness inside my slacks.

Ignoring the desire sliding through my veins, I shut her door, jog to my side, and settle in so she isn't sitting in the sizzling vehicle for too long. Turning on the ignition, I get the AC going on high and drive us back to the club.

Once I walk her to her car, she turns to face me. "Thanks for a delicious and fun lunch."

"I enjoyed it, too." A warm breeze floats through the air and a lock of hair blows across her cheek. Reaching out, I tuck it behind her ear, the tips of my fingers grazing her cheek. She shivers, a tremor racing through her, and I glance down to see her nipples, hard peaks visible through her camisole.

She tilts her head up, her lips parted in what looks like a silent request for a kiss. I stare into her eyes, and I'm so fucking tempted to cross the invisible boundary I've erected... but I can't. I wasn't smart during the early years of my life, and I've worked too hard and come too far to screw up again by kissing my business partner's sister. The woman I have to work with on a party important to both Rainey and the club I own.

Instead of taking her up on the not-so-subtle offer, I step back and open her car door. "We'll talk again soon?" I ask, knowing we have more things to do to prepare for the Thunder's year ahead.

Her cheeks are flushed as she nods. "We will." She enters the vehicle, no longer meeting my gaze.

The sexual tension is gone, replaced by her embarrassment, and I'm not happy with myself. Not at all.

CHAPTER SEVEN

Rainey

"I'M MORTIFIED," I say out loud, as I drive home from Midnight, fresh from offering myself to Lucas and being turned down.

I don't know what I was thinking. One minute we're standing by the car, the next he's tucking my hair behind my ear. I feel his knuckles against my cheek and it's like his touch engages my entire being. Next thing I know, I'm tilting my head up, all but begging him for a kiss. And the man I thought desired me as much as I do him steps back and hustles me into the car.

"How about you come over. I'll make dinner, and we can talk about how much men suck?" Kaylee offers.

I shake my head, then remember to speak. "No, thanks. I need to stop by my mom's. Dad is out with my uncle Alex for a business dinner, and I told her I'd keep her company."

"Okay, but I'm here if you want to talk."

I'm so grateful to have a friend like Kaylee.

"Thanks. See you in the morning."

"Bye." I click off the phone.

About thirty minutes later, I'm sitting in Mom's kitchen, my hands wrapped around a cup of hot tea. My mother is sitting next to me, both of us on high stools around the center island. I grew up in this house, and it holds so many good memories. At the thought, I think about Lucas and how he doesn't have a decent childhood to look back on, and my heart breaks for the hurt, angry boy he'd once been.

Am I still embarrassed by the kiss thing? *Yes.* Though I have no choice but to move past it.

"Earth to Rainey," my mom says.

I look up and she comes into view. My mother is wearing a lounge outfit in lavender, a color that suits her well. Her long hair is pulled into a low ponytail and her makeup is light, as always. She's beautiful, and not just because I'm biased.

According to the rest of the world, I'm my mom's mini-me. I think my face is a combo of both my parents. I have chocolate brown hair, like her, and curves—too many, if you ask me—also like her. I have freckles across my nose—and so does she. But my eyes are all my father's side. All the Dare siblings have dark navy eyes and so do their kids. It's a dominant gene, I suppose.

"Rainey, honey, where are you? Is everything

okay?" Mom asks.

I shake my head and laugh. "Sorry. I was lost in thought. Just thinking about whether I look more like you or Dad, and how many traits you and I have in common."

She grins. "It always makes me happy when people say they think we're sisters. Of course, it's more a compliment to me. Makes me feel younger." Mom leans in and props her chin in her hands. "But I sense there's more on your mind than whether we look alike. Want to talk about it?" she asks.

About how I'd practically begged Lucas to kiss me? No. About my appointment tomorrow? The one I've been pushing out of my mind but can no longer ignore? That, I can do. "I have a meeting at the museum tomorrow to discuss a temporary exhibit for the Thunder during the 50th anniversary season."

Mom sits up straight in her seat. "The museum?" she asks warily, and I understand why.

Adam Roberts, my ex, works there, and I do my best to steer clear of him.

I nod. "With Adam." He's the curator of the museum. "Trust me, I tried to meet with his assistant. I even had the date scheduled, but Adam had the man cancel. If I want this exhibit, I'm going to have to meet with him." Over lunch, though I doubt my mother wants to hear I'm sharing a meal with my ex, the persistent jerk.

When I thought of the idea of doing the exhibit at the museum, I'd known I'd have to deal with him. We dated for six months a year ago, and he pushed for too much, too fast. I didn't want to spend all my free time with him, while he attempted to take over my life. I'd tried to pull back and just when I decided to break up with him, he proposed. That was the final red flag. Who gets engaged in six months when his girlfriend is clearly pushing him away?

When I said no, he turned nasty, grabbing my wrist and calling me a spoiled brat who didn't know how good she had it. A stranger stopped and asked if I was okay. That shook Adam up, and he immediately pulled the *I'm contrite* act, but I didn't buy it then, nor do I every other time he surfaces, always in between girlfriends. Needless to say, meeting with him, even for an important job, doesn't sit well with me.

"Why don't you ask Kaylee to go in your place?" Mom suggests.

I sigh. "Adam made it clear if I want him to consider the exhibit, I need to be the one who comes to discuss it."

My mother's eyes narrow. "Then take her with you."

"I plan to."

Mom lets out a long breath. "You already know

this, but I grew up with an abusive father. It's the reason we created the safe haven project."

My parents helped set up Haven for Help, a non-profit that gives women a place to land when running from an abusive significant other. Or anyone, for that matter. They offer counseling, as well as being a shelter for women who need to hide and then relocate.

I nod because all my siblings are aware, and I've volunteered there many times.

"Suffice to say, I know the signs," my mom says. "The red flags. And that's not something I ever want for my daughter. And if your father knew you were meeting with Adam—"

"He can't find out," I tell her, panicking. If my dad found out, he'd storm the museum, and I'm afraid of what he'd do to Adam. "I'll be fine and I'll call you when it's over. Besides, we're meeting in a public place." Sort of.

I have no desire to meet with Adam alone and the restaurant he chose is known for leisurely dining, even during lunch hour. It's where people take clients they want to schmooze and impress with large booths and lots of privacy. None of which Mom needs to know.

"Okay." She frowns. "But I don't have to like it."

I let out a sigh of relief. "If it makes you feel any better, I don't like it either. But the exhibit will be worth an hour of my time with the jerk." Not wanting to think about the meeting anymore, I smile at my mother. "How about we eat dinner?" I ask, changing the subject.

I don't want to talk about my ex any more than I want to think about Lucas, and he's been on my mind nonstop despite the conversation about Adam.

★　★　★

THE NEXT MORNING, Kaylee calls in sick with a stomach virus.

Now, I'm sitting at my desk, drumming my pencil on the counter, trying to figure out how I'm going to handle lunch with Adam, when I make my decision. I pick up my phone and dial the museum. I'm not willing to use Adam's cell phone number. Heaven forbid the man and his huge ego think it's for personal reasons.

The main desk answers, and I ask to be put through to Adam Roberts. The phone rings twice and I hear his familiar voice. "Hello?"

"Adam, it's Rainey. Kaylee can't make it to our lunch today. I'm going to come by the museum instead." I don't want to share a meal with him and send the wrong message. It's a running theme when dealing with the man. Making sure I'm clear about where we stand at all times.

"Rainey," he says in a cajoling voice that makes my skin crawl. "That wasn't what we agreed to. You said you'd go on a lunch date with me."

This man and his gaslighting, I think to myself, shaking my head at his behavior. "I said no such thing. I agreed to a *business* lunch and now I have changed my mind. It's my prerogative," I remind him. "I want to discuss a temporary Miami Thunder exhibit for their 50th anniversary season. There's no reason to go for lunch in order to do that."

Silence, then, "What's really wrong? Are you too good to be seen with me?" he asks, a nasty tone to his voice.

I have no doubt if we were in the same room, he'd be in my space attempting to intimidate me. But I'm in my own office and I'm safe.

I pinch the bridge of my nose, debating how far to take this and decide, screw it. I'm not going to let him have the upper hand. "I'll tell you what, Adam. I can call your director and explain how his head curator won't discuss a huge opportunity for the museum and is completely unprofessional *or* we can have the conversation right now, over the phone."

"You are such a spoiled bitch. You always think you're better than everyone else. That if you snap your fingers, I'll do what you say," he says in the angry tone I only began to hear at the end of our relationship when I wouldn't go along with his demands.

I'm still shocked he'd fooled me into thinking he was a nice guy and a gentleman in the early days of dating. "Okay. Calling your boss it is." I move the phone from my ear, about to disconnect the call, when I hear him speak.

"Fine. Let's talk business."

Relieved I've won this round, I pitch my idea, knowing how much money a ticket for Thunder memorabilia will bring to the museum. Adam might want to hang up on me or berate me for his amusement, but he needs this booking and he knows it.

Thirty minutes later, I've secured the exhibit with details to be worked out at a later date. "Oh, one more thing," I tell him, then continue before he can speak. "You won't be working with me. I'll be sending someone on my team to handle things. It's been a pleasure doing business with you," I say, and disconnect the call.

Unfortunately, I would never subject another woman to Adam's difficult personality and lying charm. I wouldn't want to risk someone possibly falling for him and then seeing the creep beneath the smooth exterior when it might be too late. But *someone* needs to work closely with Adam, and it can't be me.

I could ask my father or brothers to help, but that will make them get all protective, and I've worked too hard to escape their watchful eyes to alert them to potential issues with my ex again. Which brings me to the person I embarrassed myself with yesterday.

I'm pretty sure if I ask Lucas to run interference with Adam, he'll be more than happy to do it. I just need to gather the courage to face him again.

CHAPTER EIGHT

Lucas

FRIDAY NIGHT AND the club is packed. I'm hanging with Tristan, and Jack, who is leaving tomorrow for Charleston to scope out locations for our second night club. His departure had to be pushed back due to storms there, so we have time, just the three of us.

We've been talking for an hour and I'm nursing a drink, doing my usual survey of all that's happening at Midnight. Below our level is the dance floor. I stare, taking in our guests dancing, bodies writhing against each other, and loud music keeping the mood elevated.

Suddenly, Tristan rises from his seat. "I'm heading out. I have a lady to meet."

"New week, new lady?" Jack asks, a knowing smirk on his face.

Tristan grins. "You know it. Why get pinned down by one when there are so many? Right, Lucas?"

I raise an eyebrow. I may have felt the same way a few years ago. We both have a history of not wanting to commit, and when I was younger, I enjoyed variety. But the merry-go-round of women has been getting stale for a while.

"That's not it, not anymore," I say. I want a relationship. Someone to lie down with at night and wake up beside in the morning. Mutual love and support. Things I never had as a child. "But I've just screwed up any relationship I've tried to have."

As soon as someone got close, I'd push them away. No one ever knew *me*. But Rainey does. She's already aware of more about my past than any female I've been with before. I've opened up to her, giving her tidbits of information I never wanted to share.

I don't want to get all sentimental and shit with the guys, so I say, "It's been a while since I've been with anyone." Something I haven't given any thought to.

Until Rainey. Not that I can admit as much.

Tristan, still standing, stares me down, but I'm not giving in. He may know about my feelings for Jack's sister, but he'd never betray me.

"It's been over a year, hasn't it?" he asks, serious, no teasing in his tone.

I roll my eyes. "Keeping track of my sex life?"

He lifts one shoulder. "It's so pathetic, it's hard not to," he quips back.

Jack snorts. "Look down at the dance floor. I have no doubt you could find someone to take home for the night if you wanted."

"I could say the same for you, Jack," Tristan says.

Jack shakes his head. "Don't you have plans? Just go and leave us alone," he mutters.

I understand. I have my issues with connection and Jack has his. Dumped by his fiancée, he's been picky ever since.

"At least *I'll* be having fun tonight." Tristan chuckles and walks away, headed for his one-night stand.

I shake my head. "I thought he'd never leave."

"You sure you don't want me to play wingman for you tonight?" Jack asks.

I lean back in my seat. "I'm content as is. How about you?"

"Same. I'll be busy enough in Charleston. The last thing I need is to get involved with anyone, even for one night." Jack gestures to Sophie, who always serves on this floor, calling her over.

"Hello, gentleman. What can I get you?" she asks.

"Whiskey on the rocks. You know my brand," I tell her.

"Bourbon," Jack says.

She smiles. "Be right back."

Ordering alcohol has me thinking back to Rainey and the specialty drinks Mak made for her. "So you know I met with Rainey about specialty drinks for the anniversary, right?"

Jack nods. "How'd it go?"

"Mak nailed three unique blends in one shot. Pun intended." I chuckle at my lame joke. "But your sister loved her creations. She also enjoyed the presentation." And I enjoyed the lunch we grabbed and the time we spent together afterward.

Her hair blew around her face from the breeze off the ocean, and I loved how she ate without caring what I thought. Her attitude was refreshing and only made me like her more.

"Perfect. Sorry to pass off the job on you, but Rainey's easy enough to work with," Jack says. "You'll have no problems."

Oh, I have problems, I think to myself. Problems keeping my hands to myself.

The issue would be the phone call I received from Rainey earlier today. She needs me to handle the exhibit at the museum and gave me the rundown of all I needed to know. The man in charge of the museum's role in the exhibit is her ex, Adam Roberts. Though she didn't tell me outright, I get the feeling she's afraid of him on some level. And she begged me not to tell anyone in her family, including Jack.

Which means I feel like I'm betraying my friend on two different levels.

MONDAY EVENING, THE club is closed and I'm alone with Rainey at her office. Her company is in charge of the upcoming Foster Fundraiser Charity Gala coming up soon, and her partner is running point, so Kaylee is busy tonight with the client. Rainey's family always attends, as does mine. Foster kids are important to the Dares and to the Carras family for similar reasons. Madison and Alex Dare fostered many children over the years, adopting the ones who didn't end up going home. Like me.

Rainey's receptionist is gone for the day. We've ordered Chinese food and are waiting for the delivery to arrive so we can eat while we talk.

We sit beside each other at the same table we shared the first time I came here, discussing the opening anniversary party for the team family, as she calls the invitees. Through the windows lining the wall, the sun begins to lower on the horizon, but the overheads give us plenty of light.

We've already talked about the hors d'oeuvres. Since, by law, Midnight has to serve food, we agreed to have the dinner part of the night catered by a company of Rainey's choice. Weather permitting, we'd serve food on the rooftop, using chafing dishes while hors d'oeuvres are passed around by servers. If it rains, we'll move the food inside to the lower level.

"I thought we'd hang tapestries of the current first-string players around the main room," Rainey says. "Will that work for you?"

I realize I've been lost in thought, but I heard what she said. "That's fine."

She glances up at the lights, her brow crinkled in thought. "What if we change the white string lights on the rooftop bar to the team colors?"

"We can do the lights on the roof in black and gold," I say at the same time she offers up the same idea.

The tinkling sound of her laughter echoes in the empty space. "We can check that off the list," she says with a cheeky smile. "Apparently, we're in agreement. Kaylee and I call it mind-melding."

I like that we're on the same page with things, both vibing well. It's a pleasure planning with her, discovering how her mind works and how good she is at her job.

"Is it always like this when you meet with clients?" I ask. "Because this has been amazingly easy compared to some of the people I've dealt with who rented out the rooftop for a party." Some human beings can be a royal pain in the ass.

"Well, most people aren't as fun and easy to be around as you are."

I take the compliment and let it fill me up. It isn't something I hear often. "Well, I can say the same about you."

"Thank you. But to answer your question, no, it's not always this easy." The smile that lit up her face dims. "In fact, three years ago, when Kaylee and I started the company, we were building a steady clientele until a man named Gregory Atwater hired us to do a holiday party for his investment firm. Kaylee was already working on another company's event, so I took lead on his." Rainey lets out a heavy sigh, and I can tell it's not a good story.

I wish I could reach out and pull her into my arms, but that would be beyond inappropriate, so I just listen.

"Everything he agreed to, he had an issue with the night of the party. The details aren't important but the gist of it is. He bad-mouthed not just me but our company to everyone who would listen. He even made use of online reviews to trash us there, too, always making sure to use my name." She dips her head and her eyes shimmer, showing me how badly the incident affected her.

The need to comfort her is strong. Reaching out, I place my hand over hers and we sit in silence for a few long seconds.

"It gets worse," she finally says. "Long-standing bookings canceled on us. Our phones grew silent. The business we'd been building with such high hopes and hard work came to a standstill. And I can't help but feel like it was all my fault."

If Gregory were standing before me now, it would be my pleasure to take a swing. It's one thing to be unhappy with someone you hire, another to deliberately destroy their business. My gut tells me Rainey worked hard on the event and even if some things went wrong, the unexpected always happens. But I'm sure she did a stellar job and didn't deserve the backlash she received.

"You can't blame yourself because someone else doesn't deal with disappointment in a professional way. Or because that person is an ass."

She bursts out laughing.

Goal accomplished.

"I needed that," she says, still grinning.

"I'm glad." I lean in and brush her hair off her shoulder. "I hate to see you sad," I say, realizing at that moment our lips are inches apart and this time, I'm not going to be able to stop myself from kissing her.

Her lips part, my mouth touches hers, and fucking fireworks go off in my brain. She tastes sweet, better than I've imagined, and I've done plenty of fantasizing about this very moment. I slide my hand around her neck, pulling her close as our tongues meet. She's everything I've ever wanted and if this is all I get, I'll die a happy man.

A soft moan escapes her throat, and I'm about to

pull her into my lap when glass shatters as a loud crash sounds and something comes flying through the window. I dive, pushing Rainey off the chair and onto the floor, waiting to see if anything else happens before I finally roll off her and let her sit up.

She's shaking and I wrap an arm around her, pulling her into me. "Are you hurt?" I ask.

"No. It just scared the shit out of me."

What the hell just happened? I try to stand but she grabs onto me, and I hold her for a while longer, breathing in her familiar scent, waiting until she stops shaking to release her. "Okay?" I ask.

She nods, so I stand, pull my phone from my pocket, and call 911, reporting the incident. Then, I look toward the destroyed window. I don't see anything or anyone outside. Stepping on the glass would be stupid, so I'll wait until the police show up.

I help Rainey to her feet as something dawns on me. "Why is the glass fragile enough to break? We live in a hurricane zone. You should have high-impact resistant glass." I know because we redid the windows on the building when we designed and built the club.

She winces. "The landlord is a cheap bastard on most things, and to be honest? I didn't know. Now I do."

I make a mental note to make sure that's handled soon.

The police arrive and while one officer checks the area outside, his partner questions Rainey and me. As she answers, I learn there are only cameras inside, not out, so there's no capturing the person's face. Strike one.

"Can you think of anyone who has problems with you?" the young officer, who can't be more than twenty-two or -three, asks.

She shakes her head. "I really can't."

"What about the story you just told me?" Gregory Atwood sounded like a vengeful man.

"Miss?" the officer prods.

Rainey draws a deep breath. "I had issues with a client three years ago, but I haven't heard from him since. He's probably forgotten all about me."

The cop frowns. "I can take the name, but I agree with you. It's doubtful the person's held a grudge this long. Anyone else?"

"Pete," his partner says as he joins us. Wearing thick gloves, he's holding a brick which has heavy-duty paper wrapped around it. "Check this out. It was thrown through the window." He pulls off a large, thick band and removes the piece of paper from around the brick.

In red marker, is a note. The officer holding the paper reads it aloud, then turns it around for us to see.

You don't deserve a good life. Prepare to lose everything.

Anger fuels me and I clench my fists. Who the hell would want to scare her so badly?

Rainey gasps. "I just remembered something!"

"What is it?" I ask.

"Give me a second." She rushes over to her desk, opens a drawer, removes something, and returns, handing what looks like a postcard to the police. "This arrived with the mail a couple of weeks ago, except there's no postmark. I brushed it off at the time, but something made me save it."

"Similar," the cop with the gloves says, showing his partner.

"Can I see?" I ask.

He turns the card over to me and I glance at the writing.

You think you're special but you're not. You don't deserve good things. Go away!

"Same writing, Similar message," the officer says.

The two men step aside to confer. Meanwhile, Rainey moves closer and I pull her into me, wrapping my arms around her tight. I don't want her afraid and I'll be damned if anyone hurts her. Right now, though, there's not much I can do and if there's anything I despise, it's feeling useless.

After a few minutes, the officers return, and Rainey steps out of my embrace and stands up straight, facing them.

"Okay, here's where we are," one of them says. "We'll talk to other businesses in the area, see if there are outdoor cameras that caught anything. We'll bring the brick and the notes in for evidence. But frankly, without cameras, right now, we have nothing to go on."

I scowl at the man even as I know he's right.

"Do you live alone?" the other man asks.

Rainey nods. "But my building has a doorman."

He meets her gaze. "Depending on the security at the desk, you might want to stay with a friend for a couple of days. Just until we check cameras and see what we can find out."

They talk for a few more minutes and promise to be in touch.

Once we're alone, I turn to Rainey. "I'll call a friend and get the window boarded up for tonight so you don't have to worry about everything inside."

She nods, her eyes glazed and glassy. "Thank you."

I wish I could do more. "I'm assuming you're too shaken up to drive?" I ask, knowing I won't let her even if she says she's okay.

Rainey wraps her arms around herself in a self-protective move. "You assume right."

"Then do you want me to take you to your parents' house?" I offer the only place I think she'll feel safe.

She shakes her head. "No. Dad will lose his mind, and Mom will worry too much. Can you take me to Kaylee's instead?"

"Of course. I'll take you." Though I'd love nothing more than to bring her home with me, that would cause a whole host of problems neither of us are ready for.

Besides, I'd kissed her and we haven't had time to process or talk about the step we've just taken. If she came to stay in my apartment, Jack would have questions that, again, neither of us could answer right now.

"Let me call Kaylee," Rainey says. "She needs to know what happened and I'll find out if she's home from dinner yet."

While Rainey tries to reach her friend, I get in touch with a contractor pal and arrange for him to board up the window so no one can get inside tonight. He's a good guy and promises to come right over despite the late hour.

Not wanting to leave the office empty with the windows shattered, we wait for him to arrive. I pull Gary aside. I tell him to enjoy the Chinese food that will be delivered soon, then we discuss replacing the windows with shatter-proof and hurricane-resistant glass. I don't care what it costs. Do I think Rainey will be annoyed that I stepped in? Definitely. But as long as she and Kaylee are safe, I'll sleep just fine, even if she's upset.

Still shaken, Rainey gathers her things. She gives Gary the alarm code so he can set the system and bypass the set of windows, allowing the rest of the place to be armed. She tells me she'll change the code in the morning.

With my arm around her, we walk to my SUV so I can drive her to Kaylee's, all the while wishing I was the one watching over her tonight.

CHAPTER NINE

Rainey

O N THE DRIVE to Kaylee's, my mind spins, trying to figure out who could have thrown the brick. Who sent the postcard? Who wants me to go away so badly?

"Are you okay?" Lucas asks, glancing at me before returning his gaze to the road.

I shrug. "Shaken up. I have no idea who would throw a brick through the window just to send me a message."

He reaches over and threads our fingers together. "We'll find out." He squeezes in reassurance, and it works. Instead of thinking about the incident tonight, my mind drifts back to the moment right before. Lucas and I kissed and the feeling was magical. His lips were softer than I imagined and his taste was delicious. There are no words to describe the sweep of his mouth on mine, his tongue plundering inside. Just us making that first connection I've been craving arouses my body and has my mind whirling.

My free hand drifts to my lips, and I feel the heat

of his gaze for a brief second before he rubs his thumb back and forth over the top of my hand. "We have time to sort that out," he says, reading my mind.

"I know. But it's like we let the genie out of the bottle, and I don't know what happens next." And I'm not good with things being up in the air.

"We have time," he assures me.

It's not an answer, nor does it tell me how he feels. But he's right. With everything going on in my life, I have more important things to think about. Because whoever threw that brick is escalating from sending a harmless postcard. If anyone had been standing by the window, they could have been hurt.

He pulls the SUV up to Kaylee's apartment and parks out front, then turns to me. "You have my number, so if you need anything, call me."

I manage a smile. "I will."

His gaze holds mine. "I mean it, Rainey. Any time."

I nod, grateful for him. Between his gruff tone and the reassurance that he'll be there for me, I feel warm and cared for in ways I've never experienced before from a man I'm interested in. It's not like when my dad or my brothers want to protect me. This feels more… personal. And I like it.

"Thank you. I'm glad you were there when it happened." I could have handled things myself, but having someone there when I felt so vulnerable helped. *He* helped.

"I'm glad too." He lifts the hand he's holding and brings it to his lips, pressing a kiss to my skin.

I lean toward him, across the center console, and before I realize my intent, his mouth touches mine and the kiss we'd begun earlier picks up where we left off. His tongue sweeps across my parted lips and delves inside. Sparks light up inside me and my body reacts, my nipples growing hard and my sex clenching with need. But I'm aware we're inside an SUV and nothing more than this can happen.

Still, I'm disappointed when he pulls back. "I should walk you up," he says, and I've already learned better than to argue.

"Okay." I rub my damp lower lip with my finger, and he lets out a groan before turning away to open the door.

At least I'm not the only one left frustrated and wanting, I think, as he comes up to my side of the vehicle and helps me exit.

Together, we walk up the path to the main entrance of the building where Kaylee is waiting, her eyebrows raised. "I was so worried!" She pulls me into a hug and whispers in my ear. "You'd better believe we're going to talk about that kiss."

I'm not sure how she saw from here, but I'll ask

her later, I think, as I step out of her arms.

"Come on. I'll walk you ladies to the apartment," Lucas says, pointing to the elevator not far away.

Kaylee nods at her doorman and smiles.

Once we're in front of her door, I turn to Lucas. "Thanks again for everything."

He nods. "Don't forget what I said. *Any time.*"

I know what he's referring to and smile in return.

"Be safe, both of you. Now go inside and lock the door." He gestures to the apartment with one hand.

We do as he instructs, and once in the apartment, Kaylee turns the lock, then the deadbolt. "So," she says, as she turns and leans against the door. "Talk to me."

"I told you everything that happened at the office already." Am I playing dumb? Yes. But procrastinating seems best, though I know Kaylee will get right to the point anyway.

"But I don't know about you and Lucas. Last I heard, you were mortified and going to act like offering yourself to him never happened." She raises an eyebrow. "But tonight, I go downstairs to wait for you, I see the Mercedes pull up and recognize Lucas's profile, so I start down the walkway to meet you. Except when I look in the window again, you two are making out like teenagers, so I went back inside to wait."

I frown at her phrasing. "I never said I offered my-self up to him," I mutter.

"You offered your mouth. Potato, potahto."

Unable to hold back, I let out a much-needed laugh. "Fine. We kissed. Twice. Now, can I please get something to eat, because I didn't have dinner and I'm starving."

"Luckily for you, I have leftovers from the restaurant tonight. Chicken parm and spaghetti. I am so relieved I have my appetite back and can eat whatever I want again." Though her eyes had opened wide when I said I'd kissed Lucas *twice*, she's obviously taking pity on my empty stomach.

I reheat the food in the microwave and sit down to eat, grateful for the delicious meal.

"Now, spill," Kaylee says in her most demanding tone.

"I really don't know how to explain it. We were working and getting along really well, sharing ideas. I confided in him about what happened with Gregory Atwater, and of course I was upset. He said something to make me laugh… and the next thing I know—"

"You locked lips. Yep, got it. I don't need a description."

Shaking my head at her, I grin. "That's about it."

"Well, I'm happy for you," she says, and I know, without a doubt, she means it. She's always in my corner and I'm in hers.

I hold up one hand. "Not so fast. We kissed and then the brick came flying through the window. We've had no time to talk about what it meant, if anything." Though my heart squeezes at the thought of me being just a blip on the man's list of willing women.

Kaylee purses her lips and thinks before speaking. "He kissed you a second time, so I hardly think it meant nothing to him."

"True. But I still think there are obstacles. Big obstacles like my brother. My father. Me not acting professionally if things go further."

Leaning back in her seat, Kaylee shakes her head. "Brother's best friend. Brother's business partner. Forbidden romance," she says.

"What are you talking about?"

"Romance novel tropes. I just listed three of them. They're the things that keep the hero and heroine apart," she explains.

"I forgot. You're my true crime watching, romance reading friend."

She smiles, proud of her hobbies. "Correct. So, with all my knowledge, here's what I suggest."

Having finished my meal, I push the plate aside. I'll clean before bed because I'm a grateful and neat houseguest. "I'm listening."

"Sleep with him."

"What?" I'm sure I heard her wrong.

She props her chin in her hands. "I said, sleep with him. Call it a fling until working together is over and agree you won't tell anyone who might get upset by the news. You'll both know going into it, it's not serious. That way, nobody gets hurt."

Though she's telling me about book tropes, I have to admit her idea makes sense. I haven't ended up in love with any of the men I've dated long term, so it should be easy to keep my heart safe from falling for Lucas, right? That pesky organ in my chest thumps hard, as if disagreeing with me.

"I'll think about it," I tell her. Because the idea of jumping into bed with Lucas isn't something I'll take lightly. I rise from my seat and gather my plate.

"Think about something else while you're at it. You deserve to be happy, no matter what your family or anyone else thinks."

I sigh. If only it was that easy. She didn't grow up a daddy's girl, Ian Dare's daughter who always wanted to make him proud. Sure, I'm twenty-nine years old and can make my own choices, but I'm still compelled to act as expected.

While I clean up, we talk about the brick attack, and who might be behind it, but we both come up empty.

Afterward, she turns out the lights and walks me to

the room next to hers, a pretty second bedroom with neutral colors I've stayed in before. She lends me a T-shirt to sleep in and clothes for tomorrow. Since I'm curvier than she is, I hope the leggings and top fit. Though I'm tired by the time I wash up and lay down in bed, I can't sleep. The crash of the brick through the window replays in my head and my heart pounds as hard as it did when it happened.

I think back to Lucas telling me to call him any time and pick up my cell to do just that. Except I need to think more about our two kisses and Kaylee's suggestion. As much as the idea appeals to me, I'm already too into him to keep things light and casual. Instead of calling or texting him, I toss and turn for most of the night.

When the sun streams through the window, waking me, I realize at some point in the early hours of the morning, I fell asleep. My eyes still feel gritty and I'm tired. After stretching, I pick up my phone to see it's after ten a.m. and I sit upright in bed. I overslept and Kaylee didn't wake me.

I grab the clothing she'd given me and head to the bathroom to brush my teeth and wash up, then dress and walk to the kitchen. Kaylee, dressed in the same type of casual clothing as me, is making French toast.

"Morning. Why didn't you wake me?" I ask.

She turns her head toward me. "Because I figured

you needed to rest, so I used this morning to sleep in, too. I was going to wake you once I finished these." She rotates back to the cooktop. Using a spatula, she takes the last piece of French toast from the frying pan and places it on a plate. "I made your favorite."

"It smells delicious, but you didn't have to go to any trouble."

"No big deal. Oh! Speaking of trouble, Ashlynn arrived at the office to discover a contractor was there installing new windows," Kaylee tells me.

I raise my eyebrows. "Did you call anyone first thing this morning to fix it?" Because how else would someone be working already?

She shakes her head, then places our plates on the table. She puts the frying pan into the sink and turns on the water.

"Leave it," I tell her. "I'll clean up."

She shuts off the faucet. "I won't argue with that." We take our seats at the table. She already has maple syrup and powdered sugar on the table, along with orange juice and water. "You know where the coffee is," she says, picking up her fork.

"Aren't you concerned someone is fixing our windows?" I ask.

"Nope. Because the man said Lucas Carras arranged for the work to be done." She pours syrup onto her plate, cuts off a piece of bread, stabs it with a fork, and pops the piece into her mouth.

I'm stunned speechless. "Please tell me you called in and gave the man your business credit card?" Because I don't want Lucas paying for us. Especially something so expensive.

"Again, nope. That's between you two." She points to my plate with her fork. "Eat up before it gets cold."

I shake my head and wonder what I'm going to do about the man I can't get out of my head, the man who's inserted himself into my life, all the while knowing we can't ever really be together.

Unless… I do what my best friend suggested and sleep with him for the short time we have. Stumped and too tired to keep thinking, I pick up the syrup and drown my French toast before digging in.

CHAPTER TEN

Lucas

ESPITE THE FRIGHTENING night she'd had, Rainey didn't call. I doubt she'd had an easy time or a good sleep, but at least she'd had her best friend to keep her company. I still wish it had been me taking care of her.

Instead, I lay awake, my thoughts spiraling from the brick in Rainey's window to my past ventures with Trick and the guys. We'd been assholes, no doubt, but I'd never threatened anyone. But Trick had and he'd even gone a step further, hurting an old man. If not for the notes that seemed to explicitly target Rainey, I'd wonder if it were Trick threatening her to get to me. But the wording, *you don't deserve nice things*, or *be prepared to lose everything*, that's personal.

I woke up after a few shitty hours of sleep to a surprising text from Rainey, asking if I was free to stop by her office. Even if I had plans, I'd make the time to make sure she's okay. But I have nothing on my schedule, so here I am.

I walk into the office, and the same receptionist is

seated at her desk.

At the sound of the bells over the door, she glances up. "Hello, Mr. Carras."

"Hello…"

"Ashlynn," she says.

I nod. "Ashlynn. I'm here to see—"

"Lucas, hi." Rainey steps up from behind her. "Come on back."

I follow her, too aware of the tight leggings, revealing her curvy ass. Even the top is a little tight. Since she went home with Kaylee, I assume she borrowed her clothing. I appreciate the sight and so does my dick. I adjust myself before she turns around.

We step into the room, and I see the back of Kaylee's head at her desk.

"We have a visitor," Rainey says to her partner.

Kaylee turns. "Hi, Lucas."

I nod at her. "Hi."

"Your arrival is my cue to leave."

I raise my eyebrows. "Why?" I ask.

"Because Rainey has some things to discuss with you, and I'd like to make myself scarce."

Beside me, Rainey snickers.

Despite Kaylee gesturing to the closed folding doors leading to the back room which are muffling the sound of the men working on the windows, I've already caught on to the problem. Rainey's upset with me and no doubt thinks I overstepped. I knew I'd have to face her irritation at some point. Might as well do it now.

Kaylee reaches for her purse in her desk drawer and rises to her feet. "Good luck," she says to me with a smirk on her face. "Bye, Rainey."

"Bye!" Rainey waves her fingers, an amused grin on her face.

Once her partner leaves, Rainey turns to me, her smile gone, but I'm determined to get ahead of the situation. "Before you say anything, I just wanted to make sure the job was done right, so I hired a crew I knew I could trust." Courtesy of the work on the club, I have a lot of connections for various construction-related jobs.

Rainey lets out a long breath. "Look, I appreciate you calling someone in to replace the windows. That's not the issue. The money is. Are they going to bill Golden Palm Events for the work?"

I rub a hand against the back of my neck. "I didn't tell them to, no."

She nods, then walks farther into the office, her high ponytail swaying behind her. Once there's physical distance between us, she turns to face me. "When I started this company with Kaylee, I had one goal and that was to do this on my own. I admit, I used trust fund money for the start-up, but we took out a small business loan and built the business ourselves."

I sense how important this is to her and I'm listening. Carefully, because the last thing I want to do is to step on her toes, and somehow, I think that's what I've done.

"My parents and family offered to spread the word about us to their corporate associates and friends, but that's not what I wanted. And Kaylee agreed. So as much as I appreciate the fact that you want to help by covering the cost, I can't let you do that. I have to contact the landlord." she says. "So instead of insisting, I'd appreciate it if you'd tell them to bill us when they're finished and I'll handle it."

I can't imagine the man will mind someone paying for the fix but I remain silent. I know when I'm beat. I can't take away the independence she's tried so hard to achieve. No matter how much I want to look out for her. "I respect what you're saying. No problem. I'll have them bill the business."

The tightness in her face eases, her jaw unclenching. "Thank you, Lucas. It really means the world to me. I've argued this point with my family for so long. I appreciate you respecting what I want."

I nod. "I'll always respect you," I assure her. "And support whatever you need."

She steps closer and when she reaches me, she pulls me into a grateful hug. I feel her softness press against my chest and my willpower to keep my distance begins to dissolve. I'm hanging on by a thread until she tilts her head and that thread breaks. I seal my mouth over hers. And if I thought the sparks we created were a one-time thing, I was wrong. Together, we're an explosion waiting to happen.

Her mouth is soft but determined and when I coax her lips open, she lets me in, sliding her tongue against mine. She tastes like a combination of spice and willing female, and I groan, wanting her with everything in my being. My cock is hard and desire rushes through my veins. She inspires a need in me that is beyond reason, and I can't bring myself to question it or hold back.

I cup her chin in my hand and—

"Rainey, I… Oh! I'm so sorry!"

I don't have to look to know her assistant walked into the room and caught us making out like teenagers. Rainey draws a breath and we pause, giving her a second before I take a step back, facing the wall. My obvious erection is the last thing Ashlynn needs to see.

Rainey looks past me. "She's gone, probably back at her desk. I can't believe I let us get so carried away in my office." She steps around me and groans, placing her hands over her face.

Without meeting my gaze, she walks to her desk, pulls a compact from her bag and looks in the mirror, rubbing her fingers over her kiss-swollen lips. With a shake of her head, she turns, and strides toward the entrance to her business, no doubt to talk to Ashlynn.

I know how much she prides herself on decorum and professionalism, and I hate that I've put her in a compromising position at work. Protecting her reputation means everything to her after what happened with that client in the past.

I shove my hands into the front of my slacks just as she walks back into the room. "Is everything okay?" I ask.

Cheeks flushed, she nods. "Ashlynn said she needed to leave early today. I told her to go. She's been calling out more often, which is odd because she's always mentioning how she needs money." Rainey shrugs.

I study her, trying to gauge her mood. "Look, I—"

She shakes her head. "It's fine. I shouldn't have started anything here."

I raise an eyebrow. "I think *we* started it. So let me ask you something. Other than getting caught, does that mean you regret our kiss?" What the hell am I doing? Why am I pushing for something that's off limits to me?

Her pretty navy gaze meets mine. "No," she admits. "I don't regret it."

Bells sound from the outside door, and we're interrupted again. I'm beginning to learn her office is the worst place to start anything personal. Conversation or kissing.

"Rainey?" a loud male voice calls out.

She cringes and shoots me a look I can't name. "Back here, Dad!"

Now I decipher that look.

"Why did I have to hear about someone crashing your window from Jack?" Ian Dare asks, in a combination of a paternal and pissed-off voice.

"And here we go," she says under her breath just as her father walks into the room, her mother beside him.

"Well?" Ian asks.

"Baby, calm down," Riley Dare insists, putting a hand on her husband's shoulder before turning to her daughter. "Answer your father's question," she says. "You know you should have called us!"

"Pot, kettle." Ian glances at his wife with an amused look.

Rainey sighs. "Because I knew how upset you'd both be. I didn't even tell Jack!"

"That would be me," I say with a wince. "He called this morning, and I told him."

Rainey shoots me a glare, while Ian glances at me for the first time.

"And it's a damn good thing you did tell him. My daughter should have let me know."

"Okay, enough! Mom, Dad, I'm fine. There was damage to the window, but it's being fixed. There's nothing for you to worry about."

I notice she doesn't discuss the odd notes she's received, and I'm glad I never mentioned them to Jack. I'm seeing the independent side of Rainey that must drive her overprotective father crazy. If I were a parent, I know I'd be the same way. My brain screeches to a halt. I'm stunned. *That* was a thought I'd never had before in my life. If asked, I'd say kids were a hard no for me. After the way I grew up, I'm not sure I can bring one into this world and not worry twenty-four seven about both their safety and my ability to be a good father. It's not like I had a decent example early on.

My gaze slides to Rainey and a weird sensation rushes through me, but I put it aside.

"I'm having a better security system installed here," Ian says. "I'm hiring a bodyguard to watch over you *and* you're working from home from now on. Our home."

"Dad!"

"Ian!" Riley and Rainey shout at the same time.

"Although I agree about the security system," Rainey's mom adds.

"The rest is overkill," the women tell him simultaneously.

I'm watching the family dynamic, and I can't help but smile at the warm, caring feeling I get, even with Ian's domineering demands, and experience a pang for what I missed being raised by shitty parents who didn't care if I came home at night, let alone if I had something to eat. But along with that painful reminder comes gratitude for the fact that I finally received all those things when the Carrases brought me into their home.

Knowing I won't score any points with Rainey's father, I join the conversation. "I agree. On the security system, anyway."

"Fine." Ian holds up two hands in surrender. "But you're coming for dinner one night soon," he says, pointing to Rainey. "Your mother wants a family meal."

Beside him, Riley coughs. "*He* does," she mutters, and her comment breaks the ice.

Rainey relaxes and everyone laughs. "We'll do it when Jack returns."

"Sounds good," her mother says.

A little while later, after Ian inspects the windows and talks to the workers, her parents leave.

Rainey turns to face me. "Well, now you see the overprotective side of my father."

I can't help but grin. "I've seen my dad act similarly." And by dad, I mean Matthew.

"Do *you* want me at dinner?" I ask, brushing my knuckles over her cheek and hoping she reads into my words and tone. I want to be more than a buffer between her and her overbearing but loving family.

I want what I have no right to ask for. And maybe, if Jack were home, I wouldn't push for answers. I'm walking further into trouble, and I can't seem to stop myself.

"Yeah, Lucas. I want you there with me."

I let her words settle inside me.

"Now, I have a favor to ask, and I know I'm pushing it. You didn't sign up for all this with me. I'm turning working on an event into a full-time job for you and—"

I cut her off with my finger, placing it over her lips. "What do you need?"

She releases a long breath. "Would you go with me to my apartment to pick up clothes for staying with Kaylee? I'm sure it's safe and there is a doorman, but the police scared me a little. I'd feel better if someone was with me."

"You got it," I tell her, not mentioning there isn't much I wouldn't do for her.

CHAPTER ELEVEN

Rainey

LAST NIGHT AND this morning have been a whirlwind. Between the brick, the kiss—or should I say kisses?—being caught by Ashlynn, then the visit from my parents, I'm ready to call it a day and it's not even noon. As Lucas and I step out of the elevator and turn right to my apartment, my stomach is in knots despite the doorman's reassurance nobody has come looking for me.

Reminding myself I have Lucas by my side, I put the key in the door and let us inside. Lucas steps over the threshold first and I follow.

Everything looks just as I'd left it and I breathe out a sigh of relief. "I feel ridiculous being so worried," I tell him as he steps back and shuts the door. I kick my shoes off and since I removed mine, he does the same.

"Because you were scared out of your mind the other night in a place you should feel safe." He sets his hand at the small of my back, and I shiver at his touch.

"I should be okay staying here, right?" I ask, turning to look at him.

He nods. "You should, but why don't you give it another night or two at Kaylee's?"

I bite down on the inside of my cheek, my friend's romance lesson spinning around in my brain. "Do you think I'd be safe here if someone stayed with me?" I ask him, my heart racing as I build up courage for what I'm about to do.

He raises an eyebrow at my obvious insinuation. "I suppose that depends on who the person is," he says, his voice gruff, as if he's already figured out what I'm really asking.

I step closer, placing a hand on his chest. "I'm thinking a big, strong man nobody would think about approaching or attacking. Someone who will keep me safe." I walk my fingers up his shirt until I can finger his open collar.

"Rainey," he all but growls. His body is stiff and his eyes are hooded.

"Just hear me out, okay?" I ask.

He sets his jaw and nods once.

I don't know where my courage is coming from, but I forge ahead. "We're both worried about us hooking up, right? Because of Jack? I don't want to come between the two of you as friends or business partners. And he's always warned me away from his friends."

"He's probably warned you away from me," he

mutters. "But yeah, that's one of the reasons." He grasps my wrist, stopping any further movement.

And I understand. I'm treading on delicate ground right now. I'm nervous even discussing the possibility of sleeping with the man I desperately desire. I think he wants the same thing, though I can't be certain.

But I'm not finished with my pitch, and I'm determined to keep going. "I'm also worried about being perceived as unprofessional by sleeping with someone I'm supposed to be working with. The Thunder account means a lot to me."

He inclines his head. "I'm aware of that, too. So where are you going with this conversation?" he asks, my wrist still in his grasp.

"I'm getting there. Can we agree we have chemistry? We both want the same thing but are hesitant to take things further?" God, if he tells me it was just a couple of kisses and I misread his intentions, I might dig a hole and curl up inside it.

"Keep going." His voice has grown lower. Deeper. Sexier.

"What if we agree to a short-term, private affair? Just until our time working together is over. Nobody will know except us. That solves the problem of Jack finding out because outside the walls of my apartment or yours, we'll be professional. No more kissing at work."

"Can I sneak one?" he asks, taking me by surprise, and I let out the breath I'm holding because now I know he's all in.

"That depends. When does this… affair… start?" I ask.

His thumb rubs lazy circles against the skin of my wrist, as if he already knows the answer and he's ready to take what I'm offering. It's all or nothing, I think, and do the boldest thing I can think of to give him his answer. I grab the hem of my—or should I say Kaylee's—T-shirt and pull it over my head.

I'm wearing a sheer, pink lace bra, and his gaze darkens, his jaw clenches tight, and his stare locks on my darkened, tight nipples.

I've captured his interest and his breathing grows shallow as he stares at my breasts. They aren't exactly tiny and I've never been this brave, but I've come this far—so I reach behind me and unhook the clasp. The straps fall around my arms and with a small shake, the bra drops to the floor.

"Fuck, you're gorgeous."

My cheeks grow hot.

He steps forward and lifts one breast in his hand, rubbing his thumb over my nipple until it's a hardened peak. Between my thighs, my sex is damp and desire overtakes me. I reach for the top button of his shirt, but he isn't finished. He dips his head and sucks a tight bud into his mouth. He teases me with his tongue and grazes the tip with his teeth until I'm rubbing my thighs together, seeking relief.

Slipping his free hand between us, he cups my sex in his hand. "I can feel you through the material. You're so wet." His voice is gruff and sexy.

He removes his hand and slips his fingers into the elastic of my leggings, and inside my panties, and I moan at the intimate touch. Unable to help myself, I spread my legs to make it easier for him to do his thing.

And he does.

His slick fingers rub back and forth across my folds, arousing me into a frenzy. My hips move in time to his rhythm and before I can catch my breath, he enters me with one finger, then adds a second. They pump in and out, his thumb brushing over my clit.

I grip his shoulders with my fingers and hold on tight while he brings me closer and closer to what I know will be a mind-blowing orgasm. And when he curls his fingers, hitting just the right spot, I detonate, seeing stars behind my closed eyelids as my climax hits hard and fast.

I dig my nails into his shoulders and ride out the pleasure, his name on my lips. When I finally open my eyes, I'm staring into his darkened green ones.

"You're gorgeous when you come," he says, his

voice rough with desire as he helps adjust my leggings.

A flush heats my cheeks and the cool air in my apartment, paired with my state of half undress, has me shivering. "Are we going to move this into my bedroom?" I don't know how much longer I can stand being the only one so exposed.

He holds out his hand, and I slip my palm against his. "Lead the way," he says, and I walk him to my large primary suite. I release my grip and turn to face him.

He's already undoing the buttons of his long-sleeved shirt, his gaze searing into mine.

He's wearing dress slacks and a white button-down, his usual attire when he's at the club at night. I assume he'd come to work planning to stay through the evening. He looks handsome and sexy and good enough to lick.

But first I need to rid myself of the awkwardness of being half naked. Brushing his hands aside, I undo the rest of his buttons, baring his tanned chest as I push the sides off his shoulders. Silence surrounds us, our gazes speaking louder than our voices ever could.

His shirt drops to the floor and as I begin to un-button his slacks, he slides his hand through my hair, pulling it to one side and kissing my neck. I shiver at the sensual, gentle glide of his lips. My nipples pucker and my entire body is tingling with arousal.

As I slide his zipper down, my hands are trembling. I hook my fingers into his boxer briefs and pants, lowering them over his hips. He shoves them down the rest of the way and kicks them aside, revealing his erect cock. A whimper escapes my throat and I grip his erection in my hand, sliding my thumb over the precum on the tip.

"Fuck." He grasps my wrist to stop any movement. "Wouldn't want this to be over before it begins."

I grin. "No, I wouldn't want that."

"Your turn." In seconds, he has my leggings down around my ankles, then helps me remove them, along with my panties.

Now we're both naked and on equal footing.

He lifts me into his arms and lays me on the bed, coming down on top of me. He braces his hands to lift his weight, his thick cock settled between my thighs, and the need to feel him inside me grows with each passing second.

"I need you, Lucas."

He seals his lips over my mouth, kissing me hard and deep, his tongue twining with mine. I moan into him and we're rocking against each other, the promise of more so close.

He lifts his head and lets out a curse.

"What?" I ask, afraid he's about to call a halt to a

very promising start.

"I don't have a condom," he says, the frustration in his tone clear.

Meeting his gaze, I do the second boldest thing of the day. "I got tested after my ex. And I haven't been with anyone since."

I hold my breath, aware I'm about to hear his recent sexual history. "It's been a while for me, too."

I raise my eyebrows. "Mr. Carras with the playboy rep?"

He shakes his head on a low chuckle. "Perception, not fact. And I've recently had a physical."

I exhale, aware that my next words will mean I'll be having sex without protection. With Lucas. I'll feel all of him inside me and no doubt we'll grow closer. He'll break through the flimsy walls I've tried to erect, and I have no idea how I'll handle it.

And yet I'm going ahead with what I need anyway. "I'm on the pill."

His gaze meets mine. "Are you sure?"

With his erection throbbing against my sex and heaven so very close? "I'm sure."

My answer earns me another kiss, this one hotter and wetter than the last. Then, he rises to his knees. He lifts my hands and wraps them around the headboard I fell in love with and just had to have.

"Hold on," he says.

I nod, gripping one of the wooden slats with each hand.

"So sexy." His lips brush mine. Bracing his hands on either side of my head, he drags his cock along my sex, teasing my clit with his hard shaft.

"So needy," I remind him, arching my hips.

He sits back on his knees and grasps his cock in his hand, giving it a powerful stroke before settling himself at my entrance. Just the tease of him is enough to make me moan and writhe, wanting him to fill me more than I need my next breath.

As if reading my mind, he braces his hands beside my head once more and fills me with one hard thrust.

My body stretches to accommodate him and suddenly I feel him everywhere. "Oh God." The words escape, and suddenly I need more, and I squeeze him tight inside me.

"Fu-u-ck." He draws out the word, then raises his hips and pulls out before plunging back inside.

I hang onto the slats but even so, with each slam of his hips, I move upward on the bed, grateful for the pillow behind me. We're in a synchronized rhythm, my hips lifting to meet his every drive inside me. My body is engaged, aware of his every move, but so are my emotions. Not only do I feel him physically, he's staring into my eyes and we're connecting on a deeper level.

I've never had sex without my partner using a condom before, and that, too, intensifies the sensations. I feel every thick inch of him as he drags his cock along my inner walls. His pace is fast but the experience is slow, drawn out until I'm crying out his name and urging him to hurry.

I wrap my legs around his waist and raise my hips, needing to take him deeper. "Lucas, please." I grip his back, digging my nails into his skin.

"Anything you want, Rainey."

"I want to come."

He slides a hand between our bodies and rubs my clit with his finger. Back and forth, up and down, around but not where I need the friction most.

"Oh God, Lucas. Stop teasing!" The words tumble out of me in a rush. I'm nearly incoherent except I know I'm begging for relief.

Finally, he plunges deep once, twice. The third time he shifts his hips and his cock hits my G-spot. "Lucas!" I cry out as he keeps thrusting into me, bringing me along for a soaring orgasm that makes me lose track of time and space.

I'm vaguely aware of him stiffening above me, then I feel his release coating inside me as we continue to rock and grind against one another until my climax and his subside. I'm a boneless heap on the bed and he collapses onto me but immediately rolls over, pulling me along with him so he's hugging me against his hard, sweaty body.

And nothing ever felt better.

CHAPTER TWELVE

Lucas

THE CLUB IS quiet at this hour of the morning. The overhead lights are on, no music, no people. I have time to sit and reflect. It's been a week since that life-changing time in Rainey's apartment. Rather than getting her out of my system as I'd hoped, she's now embedded even deeper under my skin. We'd connected on a deeper level, like joining our bodies had linked us emotionally. I'm not usually so sappy in my thoughts, but it's all true. I feel like she's mine and giving her up when our work is over won't be easy.

We've been too busy to get together again, but we've gotten into the habit of texting throughout the day, and she'd catch me up on the status of her work on the anniversary events. She'd received sets of logos for merch and to use on napkins and the bar glasses for Mak's drinks, along with swag and gift bags. She and Kaylee had chosen their favorite rendering. Rainey sent me all three and I agreed with their pick. Now, it's up to her father to approve.

I'd gone to my parents' for dinner but kept my relationship and feelings for Rainey to myself. I enjoyed catching up with my father's old stories from the bench in criminal court, and my mom's work with foster kids. Because of my upbringing and the home I grew up in, my father focused on the kids during sentencing in family court and on opportunities to create situations that would benefit young defendants.

He'd asked if I was coming to the gala next week, and I assured him that I was. I think about asking Rainey to be my date but remember her comment about nobody knowing we're together except us. My feelings shouldn't be hurt considering we need to keep our relationship from Jack and others, but not being able to take her out in public stings.

I'm sitting at the bar, scrolling through receipts, when my phone buzzes, interrupting my thoughts. I glance down at my phone lying on the counter.

As if she senses I'm thinking about her, Rainey's name appears on the screen and I swipe to answer. "Hey, beautiful." I pause at my words, then think, fuck it. I thought it so said it.

"Hi," she says, and I wonder if it's crazy to think I hear the blush in her tone.

"To what do I owe the call?" I'd rather hear her voice than read a text from her any day.

"I wanted to go over your meeting with Adam today."

My stomach grinds at the man's name, and I grip the phone harder in my hand. I'm looking forward to dealing with the guy who's made Rainey's life difficult and, if necessary, putting him in his place. "Don't worry. I can handle him," I assure her.

"I know you can," she says, a lilt in her voice. Her faith in me feels good. "Listen, I already messaged him a list of the items that will be on display at the museum. He's supposed to walk you around and show you the layout. He sent me a floor plan, and I'll forward that to you. Anything you think needs changing, just let me know."

"No problem."

She sighs. "I just hate him thinking he's got the upper hand, that I'm afraid to meet with him when that's not it at all. I just don't want him to think I'm sending him signals like I want to be with him. And he's the type to take a normal business meeting and turn it into *she wants to date me.*"

In truth, I'm glad I'm going in her place. I don't want her anywhere near the asshole. "He won't think you're afraid. Trust me, I'm going to handle him."

"Thanks, Lucas. I don't know how to thank you enough."

"You're welcome. Though I can think of a few ways next time we're alone." I smirk even though she can't see.

"You're a tease," she says, breathing heavier into the phone.

"But you're hot thinking about the possibilities, aren't you?" I can imagine her on her knees, ready to part those luscious lips and suck my cock. Or, I have a real-life vision of her laying on the bed, legs parted, ready for me to feast.

She lets out a chuckle but it's low and sexy. I hear the entry door open and see Tristan walk inside. "Okay, change of subject," I tell her.

"How about the charity gala? Kaylee tells me it's going to be a huge event and it should raise a good amount of money for the Foster Fundraiser." She sounds excited by the prospect.

"I'm glad. I intend to make a large donation myself. I know how important it is to find families willing to take in kids. Especially the difficult ones. Like me."

"My aunt Madison and uncle Alex taught me how important it is to give back. I admire them so much. Your parents, too."

I smile. "Same. I wouldn't be the man I am today without them." I pause to clear my throat. "Hey, want to be my date to the gala?" The words are out before I can stop them or think them through.

Silence follows and I'm left holding my breath while I wait for an answer. One, based on our agreement, I'm sure will be no.

"I'd love to. I want to. But we said we wouldn't go out in public like a couple."

Her first words mean more to me than any agreement we've made. "But we didn't say we couldn't be seen together as friends."

"Good point, Mr. Carras. In that case, sure. Let's go together."

I feel like I won the lottery. "Great." I pull my phone away from my ear and check the time, then return the phone to my ear. "Listen, I've got to go so I'm not late."

"Good luck and thanks again."

Forty minutes and a lot of traffic later, I arrive at the museum. The director sends me to the offices in the back. As I reach the hallway, a guy walks through the entrance, and I recognize him immediately from when Rainey brought him into the club. He has a preppy look with his blond hair and blue eyes. The arrogant tilt to his head is all his own.

"Adam," I say.

"Lucas Carras?"

He's been introduced to me before, but I play along. "Yes, that's me." I extend my hand for a shake, and he gives me the too-hard-trying-to-impress-me handshake that's utterly ridiculous. He's just pissed Rainey isn't here and unsure of why she's sending *me*, a man, in her place.

He adjusts his jacket. "I'm not sure why Rainey can't do her job herself, but let's get moving."

"She's busy," I tell him, because I know better than to antagonize him with what I really want to say: *You're an asshole and she doesn't want to be near you.*

He frowns and walks to a separate section of the museum where there are empty cases waiting to be filled. "This is where we'll hold the exhibition. I already sent Rainey a floor plan, so if you're happy with the room, we can call it a day."

I raise my eyebrows. "I was told you'd walk me through which items will be placed where so I can get a feel for the actual presentation."

"I'm supposed to believe a nightclub owner knows anything about museum exhibit layouts?" he asks in a haughty tone.

And I've had it. "Okay, look. I know you love giving Rainey a hard time because she turned down your proposal, and now you're acting like an unprofessional ass since she opted not to bow to your lunch and meeting demands. But you can't intimidate me, so don't bother trying."

"Is she sleeping with you?" He looks down his nose at me. "Because you know she'll come running back to me eventually."

I want to shake the guy and maybe put him through the wall. I tried to keep things professional, but he crossed a line. "I know she wants nothing to do with you. Now, I'm here to do a job and you're going to show me around as planned."

He opens his mouth to say something, but I step closer. "Or I can report to the museum director that I'm having an issue with his head curator." I repeat the line Rainey told me worked to get him to back off.

"Fine." He clenches his jaw and storms off, assuming I'll follow. Which I do.

Apparently his job is important to him because we spend the next thirty minutes doing the walk-through and he's a complete professional… if I ignore the scowl on his face.

After the last exhibit case discussion, I'm ready to be away from his attitude, his heavy cologne, and his company. "I'll talk to Rainey, and I'm sure she'll touch base. *By phone*," I emphasize.

Turning, I take two steps when I hear, "She's a real firecracker in bed, isn't she?"

I pivot and take two steps toward him, ready to lift him by his shirt with one hand and punch him in the jaw with the other. But that would ruin Rainey's business with the museum, so I clench my fists and breathe in slowly in an attempt to calm down.

"She didn't know how to treat me the first time around, but when she comes crawling back, I'll make sure she's learned her lesson."

His words resonate in my brain and I'm reminded of the brick through her window. Could Adam be behind the threats?

I meet his gaze with the stony glare I'd perfected when I was a pissed-off teen, one I rarely use anymore, but this son of a bitch deserves it. "Stay the fuck away from her."

Before he can reply, I turn and walk away, refusing to give him another second of my time.

I don't head back to the club right away. First, I call Rainey and update her about how the meeting went. I assure her all is well. No need to give her anything to worry about. Then, I give Tristan a call and ask him to meet me at the gym. I need to work off my anger from meeting with Rainey's ex and talk through whether Adam could be responsible for the brick thrown through her window.

Later that afternoon, at the gym, I'm sweaty from warming up and ready to work out my frustrations.

Tristan takes hold of the punching bag while I begin some boxing combos. "So today with the ex didn't go well?" he asks. I'd told him about my morning when I called him to meet me here. And he already knew about the brick at Rainey's workplace.

"He was a pompous ass. But he also said something that's bothering me about making sure Rainey learns her lesson." I throw a one-two punch at the bag, pretending it's Adam's face.

"Do you think he's behind the postcard and the brick?" Tristan asks.

I think through the wording on the threats, and I'm forced to shake my head. "The notes don't fit. They focus on her not deserving good things and being prepared to lose everything. I wouldn't rule him out, but it seems like he's more focused on getting her back than making her miserable." Neither of which would be happening.

"You're worried about her."

I raise an eyebrow. "Aren't you?"

"Sure, but not in the same way you are. So, how's it going?"

I hesitate to tell him about me and Rainey. Not because I don't trust him, but I don't want to put him in the middle of me and Jack should the truth come out. Instead, I go at the bag again.

"Hey. Lucas." His stern tone of voice captures my attention and I look up. "Tell me."

"We're working together for her Thunder party. We're getting to know each other better, too." I hold up my hands, and he unstraps each glove so I can pull them off myself. I lay them on a nearby bench and take a seat. This conversation requires my attention so I take a break from throwing punches.

Tristan leans against the wall beside me.

"She doesn't want anyone to know we're involved.

Whatever happens is after hours. I asked her to go with me to the Foster Fundraiser event, and she said we can go together. As friends."

"Ouch."

I raise one shoulder. "I try and tell myself it's not like that. The chemistry is off the charts. But…"

"Jack."

I nod. "Jack. And Rainey is very careful about her reputation. She's afraid if people find out we're sleeping together, she'll be seen as unprofessional in her industry."

"I don't get how." Tristan pushes off the wall and sits down beside me.

"Well, she had a client who was unhappy and bad-mouthed her until other companies stopped calling. She and Kaylee did rebuild their business, but it wasn't easy. So, now, being professional and doing the right thing is important to her." And I respect Rainey's work ethic.

I just wish it didn't impact us.

Hell, I'm willing to go up against Jack if it means winning Rainey in the end, but that is the last thing she wants. And I've yet to figure out another way to get through to her. Except by letting her see how good we could be together. By showing up. Being there. No matter how often she pushes me away.

"Sounds complicated," Tristan says.

I nod. "It is. But she's worth it."

CHAPTER THIRTEEN

Rainey

"*A*RGH!!" I SET my phone on the desk and lower my head to my arms.

I'm furious. I've been on the phone with the vendor I ordered the tapestries of the players from for the Thunder event at Midnight. The plan was to hang them around the club the night of the launch event—the party for the team, their families, and those who work in the front office. Then we'd repurpose them for the stadium this year.

This morning, I called to confirm the delivery date and was told I'd canceled, and my deposit will not be refunded. They were upset as it was a big job and they'd scrapped the work they'd already done. The rush job I'd paid extra for. I'm pissed because they refuse to reinstate the order even though I swore to them I didn't cancel.

Why would I? The party is in a few weeks, and they're supposed to be the *oh wow* part of the event when everyone walks in. I planned to have a spotlight over each one.

And now it looks like I'll need to start over and brainstorm new ideas. I'd found a specialty company for the tapestries and there isn't someone else to do them from scratch. Not to mention no refund means a huge hit to my budget. And I refuse to ask the client, aka my father, for more money. I have no idea how this happened or what I'm going to do to replace the tapestries.

"Are you okay?" a familiar and welcome masculine voice asks.

I lift my head to meet Lucas's concerned gaze.

"No, I'm not." I tell him about the issue with the canceled order. "And I swear to you, I did not cancel, so I don't know how this happened." My frustration level is high, and I don't know what to do.

"I believe you." His brow is furrowed like he's deep in thought.

"What is it?" I ask.

He props a hip on my desk. "Could someone have called pretending to be you and canceled the order?"

I blink a few times at the suggestion. "Why in the world would someone pretend to be me and mess up my order?"

He lifts a shoulder. "Why would someone throw a brick through your window?"

I open my mouth, then close it again. "I would never have made that connection on my own."

"I'm not saying that's what happened, but given the threats you've received about not deserving good things and preparing to lose everything? It sounds like a possibility." He lets out an annoyed groan that sounds as exasperated as I feel.

I nod, knots twisting in my stomach at the possibility. "I have two choices. I can sit here and dwell on whoever has issues with me or work on fixing the problem. I opt for fixing it."

He shoots me an appreciative look and smiles.

"What?" I ask, uncertain what that sexy tilt of his lips means.

He reaches out and strokes the top of my hand, my skin tingling where he touched. "You're strong and I admire that about you."

"Thank you," I murmur.

"And don't worry. You'll figure things out. Is Kaylee around to brainstorm?"

I shake my head. "She went out to get coffee."

"Well, that leaves us. Where do you want to start?" He unbuttons the cuff of his shirt and begins to roll up one side, revealing those strong, tanned forearms, then does the same to the other.

But I push my admiration aside. It's who he is at his core that affects me more. His compassion and caring nature are as sexy to me as his gorgeous face and scrumptious body. Even more so. "Thank you," I tell him.

"For what?" He looks genuinely perplexed.

I rise to my feet and walk around the desk, stopping in front of him. "For being here. You have your own business to run and my problems are just that. Mine. Yet you're at my office and asking how you can help."

He slides a hand along my cheek, cupping my face in his hand. "When are you going to get it? I care about you. And that means I want to see you succeed. So what can I do?"

"Well, I need to figure out how to replace the tapestries with something that is capable of being produced in a short period of time." I'm grateful to put my mind to work because thinking of anything else, such as who is trying to sabotage me, will put me on edge.

He runs a hand over his face. "You need large, blown-up pictures of the players."

I nod. "I need… banners!" The idea flies from my mouth before it's fully formed in my brain.

He nods slowly. "That could work."

"I mean, they won't be as impressive as the tapestries, but I know they'll arrive on time." Am I as passionate about them as I was about my first concept? No. But I'm in no position to complain. I just need to focus on getting the job done well.

"You know," Lucas says, glancing up at the recessed lighting above us. "If you wanted to keep a spotlight shining on each, like you'd originally planned, you still can."

"Basic, yet brilliant! We make quite a team."

"We do." He grins at me and I'm drawn into his green-eyed gaze.

Rising to my feet, I act on impulse and wrap my arms around his neck. "Lucas Carras, I appreciate you."

"Same goes, Ms. Dare." Our lips meet, and the kiss isn't hot and rushed, it's more intense and real. There's feeling beneath the physical act and butterflies take flight inside my belly.

I try reminding myself that we're in a temporary arrangement that can't go any further, but nothing about being around him, working with him, or even kissing him seems short term. He feels like a guy I can rely on. Like *my* guy.

Just as his tongue slides over my lips, I hear the tap of high heels and a chuckle. I step back from Lucas and glance toward the office entrance.

"Hello!" Kaylee places the four-cup coffee holder on her desk and waves. "No need to stop on my account." Grinning, she pulls first one coffee, then another from the holders. "Wish I'd known you were here, Lucas. I'd have gotten you one." She sits down at her desk and busies herself with who knows what.

He chuckles. "I think I'll let you ladies get back to work." He leans in close. "I'll pick you up for the gala on Saturday night. And I'll text you the time, *friend.*" He stands tall and grins, then strides past Kaylee's desk. "Bye, Kaylee."

She treats him to another finger wave. "Bye, Lucas."

I shake my head and walk back around to my desk chair and sit down.

"What was he doing here?" she asks me.

I blink and realize I don't know. I'd just been having a mini meltdown, looked up, and there he was. "He was… in the neighborhood," I tell her.

Across from me, Kaylee grins and busies herself with work on her desk.

My phone rings.

I see it's Jack and groan but swipe to take the call and put the cell to my ear. "Hi, Jack. What's up? Aren't you in Nashville?" I ask.

"And that means I can't call and say hi to my sister?" he asks.

I roll my eyes, knowing in Jack-speak that probably means checking up on me. "Of course not. How are you?" I open my laptop and make some notes regarding the banners and places I think can get me the items in time.

"I'm good. Scoping out places, meeting new people," he says.

"Anyone special?" I can't help but ask. My brother is more of a relationship type of guy, but he's never found *the one*, so my asking isn't about ribbing him, it's a serious question. I want him to be happy. If he hasn't found anyone here, maybe there's someone at one of the places he visits.

"I don't have time for romance. I'm here to work," he says in a gruff voice.

"That's not the Jack I know and love. Promise me you'll keep an eye open?"

"Sure. How are things going there? Is Lucas taking good care of you?" he asks.

If only he knows just how good. Uncomfortable with the thought, I shift in my seat. "Lucas has been great. I've had some unfortunate snags with the orders for the anniversary party and he's been a rock."

"I know he had his issues growing up, but he's a great guy and solid partner. I'm glad he's being a good friend for you too." I hear Jack's name being called. "Rainey, I have to run. I'll see you when I get home. Good luck with everything."

"Thanks! Bye." I disconnect the call and sigh.

Just what I needed from my brother. A reminder that Lucas shouldn't be anything to me but a good friend when I think of him as so much more.

CHAPTER FOURTEEN

Lucas

I DRIVE BACK to the club. It's drizzling so I turn on my wipers, but not even the rain can ruin my mood. Despite the friendship agreement I made with Rainey, we're good for each other. I know it, and so does she.

As I pull into my parking spot, I notice a bulky man with long hair, his hands in his jeans pockets, wearing a T-shirt, loitering at the entrance. There's something familiar about him but as I exit my vehicle and walk his way, I don't recognize the black tattoo sleeves on his arms, and I'm sure I'm mistaken. I've never met him before.

I tap my key fob and lock the door, then approach him. "Excuse me. Can I help you?"

He turns and I stop short. "Trick?" My stomach twists with memories best forgotten.

His familiar gray eyes meet mine. "Here he is. Mr. I've Moved Up in the World." He extends his arm and steps forward.

Next thing I know, he pulls me in for a brotherly

hug and slaps me on the back. I work out. I'm solid, but he's pure muscle, no doubt from lack of anything else to do but exercise.

I return the gesture with a slap of my own, wondering if he's being genuine or setting me up in some way.

He backs up and looks me over.

I do the same.

"It's been a while," he says, calmer than I've ever seen him. The Trick I knew was a teenage drug user and an addict, always on edge and impulsive in the worst ways.

"Sure has. I heard you were out." Might as well deal with the elephant in the room.

"It's been a couple of weeks." He looks around, then up at the sky. "The world's changed but the great outdoors hasn't." He takes a full breath of fresh air. "Feels good, man."

"I bet."

"You going to invite me in? Show me what you've done with the place." He tips his head toward the club and despite my agitation, I decide to let him inside.

I pull the door and it swings open. Since it's unlocked, either Tristan or my managers are here. The thought gives me comfort.

We walk into the club, and I know what Trick sees. A high-end establishment that tells him I've made it.

I've got money. My nerves ratchet up and I'm relieved to see Mak doing her thing behind the bar, and Tristan sitting on the other side, his laptop open.

At the sound of our entrance, Tristan lifts his head. "Morning."

"Hey."

Trick follows me toward where Tristan is sitting.

Drawing a deep breath, I begin introductions. "Tristan, this is Trick Henderson, Trick, one of my partners, Tristan Hayes."

Tristan's eyes flare for a moment, obviously recognizing the name, before he reins in any emotion and extends his hand. "Nice to meet you."

Trick steps around me and shakes his hand. "Same."

I'd introduce Mak, but I don't want to draw his attention to the pretty woman behind the bar.

Trick turns toward me. "Can we talk?" he asks.

I give Tristan a subtle nod.

He closes his laptop and rises to his feet. "I have a few things to do in the back," he says, and I know he'll be nearby if I need him.

Mak meets my gaze, then follows Tristan away from the bar.

I don't offer Trick a drink. One, I doubt his parole officer would like it, and two, I'm better off getting him out of here as soon as possible. "You wanted to talk?" I ask him.

Trick shoves his hands back in the front pockets of his jeans. "I just wanted to check in. Tell you no hard feelings."

I narrow my gaze. It can't be that easy.

"Hey, I see you're not buying it but, I swear, man, it's true. For years, I held on to my anger, but I started going to NA while I was inside. Never thought the old make amends thing was for me but…" He lifts his shoulders. "It works. I was older and you looked up to me. I liked the feeling, you know? But I led you down a shitty road. And I'm sorry."

I'm floored. Never thought I'd hear those words come out of Trick's mouth. Watching him now, his chill behavior, his sincerity, I want to believe him. "I'm happy for you. Glad the program is working."

He nods. "I got a job at a gas station. I'm living in a halfway house for now. I knew better than to go back to where I came from."

"I hope things work out for you," I say. "I never wanted to turn you in," I tell him. My mind goes back to the day Matthew Carras told me I had no choice if I wanted to stay with them, and my stomach churns the same way now as it did then.

"But you landed with good people," Trick says. "You got lucky and you got out. Ain't nothing wrong with that." He pauses, then says, "I'm going to make it, too."

And damn if I don't believe him.

We part ways and I doubt I'll see Trick again, but my heart is lighter having talked to him. Over time, I know his visit will help me come to terms with my role in his imprisonment and the guilt I've lived with, despite him ending up where he belonged. He has a second chance, and I hope he takes it.

Tristan walks back to the bar and pulls up a seat beside me. "Everything okay?"

"Yeah. He came to make amends."

My friend raises an eyebrow. "Seriously?"

I laugh. "Your expression mirrors what I was thinking when he said it, but apparently he's working the program."

"You believe him?" Tristan asks.

I nod. "Until I have a reason not to."

He braces a hand on my shoulder. "I'm here if you need me."

"Appreciate it," I tell him. "I'm going to take off for the afternoon." I decide to visit with my dad and fill him in on my visitor. I think he'll want to know Trick showed his face, but as a retired judge, he'll also appreciate that Trick is trying to do right with his freedom. "I'll be back before we open tonight."

"Take your time."

I head back to my car, buckle up, and pull out of the parking spot. I call my mom, who answers on the first ring.

"Hi, honey. How are you?"

I smile at the sound of her happy voice. "I'm good. You?"

"Just fine. I was just about to go out and run some errands."

"Oh. Then is Dad around? I wanted to stop by and talk." It's been a while since I'd seen them face to face. We speak often and I know they'll be at the gala but after seeing Trick, I feel the need for family.

"Your timing is perfect. He just got back from a morning round of golf. I'll let him know you're coming. And I'll wait to leave so I can give you a hug before I go."

"That sounds great," I tell her as I turn onto the turnpike and drive to the place they bought after Dad retired. They downsized to a still large house in Coral Gables. Which is why I was so shocked when I walked into their mansion after my biological parents passed away. The enormity of the house compared to the shack I'd lived in had floored me. I never thought people with money would want kids from a shit neighborhood to dirty their floors. I couldn't have been more wrong.

Jacinda had been unable to have kids and they'd fostered, children rotating in and out. Until me. For reasons I've yet to understand, I came, stayed, and they adopted me. I'm certain I was the biggest pain in the ass they'd dealt with, but we clicked. Matthew was the first man I learned to respect. And Jacinda's were the first arms to hug me with love.

I pull into the driveaway, careful not to block my mother's side of the garage so she can do her errands, and cut the engine. I'd stopped on the way to pick up her favorite coconut patty candies. I grab the bag, exit my car, and stride up the walkway, passing the pink hibiscus my mother favors.

Before I can ring the bell, she opens the door. Her short blonde hair is pulled back in a low clip and she's wearing a floral dress and sandals, looking as attractive as ever. In my eyes, she outshone all the other moms when she picked me up from school because she didn't trust me to come straight home.

Greeting me at the door, she pulls me into the hug I've been craving, and I return the gesture, before stepping back and leading me inside.

I'm happy to get out of the oppressive heat. "I brought you a present." I hold up the bag and she claps her hands.

"You shouldn't have! But I'm so glad you did." She grabs the gift and waves for me to follow her past the entry and into the great room across from the kitchen. "Matthew! Lucas is here!" she yells because no doubt Dad is watching golf on television at a loud volume.

I hear Dad before I see him, the tread of his foot-steps announcing his arrival. He joins us. He's wearing a pair of cargo shorts and a light blue polo short-sleeved shirt. His hair is graying at the temples but both my parents are fit and active.

"Hi, son."

I smile at the word. It never grows old. "Hey, Dad." We exchange brief hugs.

"To what do I owe this visit?" he asks. "Sit," he instructs.

"Mom, would you mind staying? I think you'll want to hear this story."

She and Dad exchange glances. "Of course," she says.

Once everyone settles into a seat, Dad beside Mom, I lean forward in my club chair. "You won't believe who came to visit me today."

"Who?" Mom asks.

"Trick showed up at the club."

Her eyes open wide, and Dad stiffens before he asks me, "You're okay?"

I nod. "I got a call a couple of weeks ago. He was released. The news left me on edge, but when I didn't hear from him, I forgot all about him until he showed up today."

"What did he want? Is there going to be trouble?" Dad asks.

"Surprisingly, no." I repeat the conversation I'd shared with Trick. "I believe he means it. He wants to change. Live a decent life." I glance at my parents' stunned faces. "I knew you'd want to hear the news in person. But there's another reason I came by."

"We're listening," Dad says.

I rub my hands together and despite being uncomfortable, because I'm not an emotional guy, I need to tell them what Trick's visit stirred up. "I never thanked you. At least, I don't think I did. Not the way I should have. You took in a troubled kid, gave him a home and something else he'd never had. Love."

"Oh, Lucas. You gave us something we desperately wanted."

I clench my fists as I ask, "Why me? You had plenty of kids coming through before me. So… why did you want to adopt me? It couldn't be because I was the easiest of all." I try for levity, but they shoot me a serious look that says I failed.

"I can answer for me," Mom says. "You needed me. Don't get me wrong, all the kids I've been lucky enough to have in my home have needed me. Us. But I sensed I could help you in different ways. I took one look at your angry, hurt, confused face and I wanted to give you everything you missed out on for as long as you'd let me. And I wasn't thinking until you aged out. I meant as my son."

A lump rises to my throat and stays there. Once I dropped that angry, hurt, confused shield she'd mentioned, I wanted everything she could give. I sensed a connection and now they're just Mom and Dad.

"As for me, maybe it was the judge in me, but I saw the path you were headed down and I wanted to alter it for you. And then I wanted to see the man you would become. Also, as my son."

Mom smiles. "I think what we're both trying to say is we felt a connection to you and a need to make it permanent."

"I felt it too," I manage to say. "After seeing Trick, I needed to come here. To thank you for changing my life before it was too late. Before I had to spend time in prison like he did."

Mom pulls a tissue from a box on the long table behind the sofa and blots her eyes. "Now come here. And don't thank us for something that was meant to be." She extends her arms toward me.

I rise to my feet, and a hug fest follows. I don't normally get emotional, but I needed this and my parents deserve to know how I feel about them.

"I'll tell you what you can do for me, though," Mom says, crumpling the tissue in her hand. "Find yourself a nice woman, get married, and give me some grandbabies."

"Jacinda! Leave him alone." Dad stands, walks over to me, and slaps my shoulder. "Ignore your mother. You do things at your own pace. But expect some hassling from your mom if you don't hurry it up."

I let out a laugh. "It's funny but when I was young, there were just so many women in my view, especially after we opened the club. But the last couple of years, I've been selective but haven't made any relationships work."

"You've had a relationship? I've never met anyone!" Mom sounds insulted.

I shake my head. "That's because there's been no one I've wanted you to meet."

Until now. I think about Rainey, how well we click, how she fits in my life in ways I didn't understand I needed. Except there's Jack. Her family. And my past standing in my way. And since I've come here to open up, I might as well go one step further.

"Can I ask you something?"

"Shoot," Dad says.

Thanks to my partnership and friendship with Jack, they know the Dares. I'd met Jack when I was still in between sneaking out and causing trouble for my parents and the incident with Trick and the guys that changed everything for me.

"You know Ian and Riley Dare pretty well, right?"

"Of course. Problems with Jack?" Dad asks.

"Not in the way you're thinking." I rub my hand over the bottom of my face, feeling the stubble from lack of shaving. "I know they had issues with me back when Jack and I became friends."

Mom's gaze narrows. "That was a long time ago."

"I've been working closely with Rainey." I leave it there, hoping one of them will put two and two together and not make me spell out my concerns.

Mom shakes her head. "You've grown up. There's no reason for them to have a problem with my son dating their daughter. Is that what's happening?" she asks, excitement in her voice, and I realize my mistake immediately.

I should have kept my mouth shut. "No. Not… yet. And I'd appreciate it if you kept any hint of a relationship to yourself."

"Got it." Mom mimics zipping her lips and throwing away the key.

"Son, it's time you start thinking about yourself as the man you are and not the troubled kid you once were." Once again, Dad puts his hand on my shoulder. This time he squeezes. "Trust me on this one."

I nod and decide not to mention Jack, and how I've already violated bro code. On a generational level, I think that's a step beyond what they'd understand.

By the time I leave and head back to the club, a

part of me feels better about pursuing Rainey for real. But not the part that's worried about my best friend and partner finding out.

For now, though, Jack is out of town, and I have Rainey to myself.

CHAPTER FIFTEEN

Lucas

I'M BACK AT the club and the night is in full swing. We're packed inside, with a line out the door and around the building. It's everything we dreamed of when we discussed opening Midnight. I look toward the bar, and a hot redhead catches my eye. I don't have a glimmer of interest in return. Though I smile, I shake my head. She shrugs and turns to the guy seated next to her.

An argument breaks out on the floor to my left, capturing my attention. I brace my hands on my chair, ready to head down the stairs from the balcony, when a bouncer steps in.

Suddenly, two hands cover my eyes. "Good job turning down that pretty woman at the bar," a familiar, sultry voice whispers in my ear so I can hear over the music.

My dick immediately hardens because Rainey is here, her amber scent filling my nostrils. I grasp her wrists and pull her hands off my eyes, then release her. "Come sit."

Grinning, she takes the chair beside me and slides in close. Because we're used to leaning in to hear each other, nobody will think anything of her nearness.

I take in her club attire. A flirty, short, teal-colored dress, cinched at the waist, then flaring out and ending mid-thigh, along with a pair of nude pumps that no doubt have red soles on the bottom. She's fucking gorgeous and she came to see me.

"What brings you by?" I ask.

"I missed hanging out with you." Her honesty surprises me. "That, and you never said why you stopped by the office this morning."

I laugh at her reply. "You could have called or texted me to ask."

"I could have." Amusement dances in her eyes. "Except…"

"You missed me," I say. "Well, it just so happens I came by earlier because I missed you too."

Her red lips part softly and I'm dying to kiss her. But we're in public and that could get us in trouble.

She rests her hand on my thigh beneath the table where no one can see and moves her palm higher, way too close to my cock that's now throbbing with desire. "Do you have to stay here all night?" she asks. "Or can we sneak out to your place or mine?"

I could probably leave and let the managers handle things. They've done it often. But I don't think I can wait for a drive to get her alone. "I have a better idea. Follow me." I rise from my seat, hoping nobody looks down and notices my erection.

I'd love to take her hand as we make our way through the club, but again… someone might notice. I hate this fucking secrecy shit, I think, as we weave through the crowd, ending up at the entrance to the back hall where the offices are located. Mine is the first one and I pull her inside, slam the door shut, and lock it behind us.

"The good news is we soundproofed the offices so that we don't hear the loud club when we're working at our desks. Scream all you want. Nobody will hear you."

Before I can think about my next steps, she's in my arms, her mouth is on mine, and all is right in my world. I kiss her, my tongue delving through her parted lips and drinking in all that is Rainey. Somehow, we end up with her back against the door.

I slide my hand up her bare thigh, feeling her silky skin, my fingers tracing the edge of her panties before slipping beneath the elastic. She spreads her legs, giving me easier access. But it's not enough and as skimpy as they are, I yank them off her, ripping the sides and shoving them into my sport jacket pocket.

"Lucas!" she squeals. "How am I getting out of here with no underwear?"

"I'll follow you out so no one can see from behind. Now hush and let me get back to what I was doing." I slip my fingers beneath her dress, finding her soaking wet. "Fu-u-ck." The word comes out on a drawl as I feel her perfect pussy.

She wraps her arms around my neck and holds on. I ease one finger inside her and pump in and out, picking up an easy rhythm. Her walls clench around me and I'm coated in her wetness, my own orgasm threatening to overwhelm me, but I'm determined to be inside her when I do.

At her little moan, I add a second finger. She whimpers and I fuck her, pumping in and out, swallowing the sighs of pleasure she gives. Her legs begin to shake, and I'm worried she won't be able to stand much longer, so I curl my fingers and rub against the spot I hope will take her over the edge.

I want to feel her come on my hand. I need to hear the sounds she makes when she climaxes. Mostly, I want to watch her expression when I make her soar.

She's shaking and I lean in to lick her jawline. "Come hard for me, beautiful."

I press my fingers harder against her inner walls and she lets out a glorious cry, her sex squeezing my fingers as she comes. I slow down, milking her orgasm for as long as I can and when I know she's finished, I undo my slacks, and shove them down along with my boxer briefs, freeing my dick that now stands erect.

"Tell me you want me," I demand, needing to know she's as desperate to feel me inside her as I am to be there.

She wraps her fingers around my erection and squeezes, sliding her hand up and down, then rubbing her thumb over the head of my cock. "I want you to fuck me, Lucas."

I lift her up by her waist, keeping her back pressed to the door, and do as she asked, jerking my hips up and letting out a low groan. "You're perfect," I tell her, as I fill her completely. We're in sync in more ways than physically.

Our gazes lock and for as often as I've had sex in my life, this is so much more. All I can see, feel, and hear is Rainey, her gorgeous indigo eyes, her gasps and moans, and the sensory experience of true passion and an oncoming explosive orgasm.

"Oh, God, I'm going to come again," Rainey cries out.

"Do it now," I grit out, hanging on, waiting for her.

I thrust my cock once, twice, and her screams hit my ears at the same time I come so hard I see stars, her orgasm prolonging my own.

A few seconds pass in peaceful quiet but for our heavy breathing until Rainey breaks the silence. "Oh,

God. That was…"

"Yeah," I say. It was." I'm still inside her and take my time pulling out and losing her warmth.

"I'm a mess," she says, her vulnerable gaze meeting mine.

I pull on my pants and walk around my desk, picking up a box of tissues. Returning to her, I carefully clean her up, aware of the flush on her cheeks as we pull ourselves together.

I cup her cheek in my hand, forcing her eyes to meet mine. "I'm glad you came by."

"Me too." Her lips lift in a soft smile.

"I was going to suggest we sit upstairs and have a drink," I tell her. "But…" I pat the pocket holding her panties, unable to hold back a grin.

"Yeah. No panties. That wouldn't be comfortable," she says, her blush now a full-on red.

"Then I'll walk you out as promised." Leaning in, I kiss her long and hard before covering her back as we head through the club and outside to her car.

I make sure she's safely inside, her doors locked before turning and walking back toward the long line and busy crowds inside.

I have a job to do and though I'm watching the goings-on at my club, my mind is solely on Rainey. She surprised me tonight by showing up at the club. Asking if I could leave so we could be alone? That gives me hope she thought about me as obsessively as I thought about her. Going along with office sex? That was mind-blowing and shocking for a woman trying to be perfect at everything she does because she cares how she's perceived in business. That means she trusts me.

And I'm not going to complain about that.

CHAPTER SIXTEEN

Rainey

I STEP BACK and look in the full-length mirror in my bedroom. The red dress I'd chosen with purpose flows around my legs. As the story goes, my mom wore a similar gown the first time my father laid eyes on her. Of course, she'd come with my uncle Alex and he and my dad weren't friends or even willing half-brothers at the time. But all that changed, and we are a close-knit family now.

When I'd seen the gown in the boutique, all I could think about was the story of my parents' first meeting, I couldn't resist. Somehow my mom had found her happily ever after and here I am doing… I don't know what.

I couldn't stop thinking about Lucas so I showed up at the club the other day with nothing but honesty on my mind. I missed him. I can't say I expected to have sex in his office, but it had been amazing. We have a connection I didn't expect and for the time we have, I intend to enjoy it.

For tonight, I want to blow his mind with this

dress. The slit up my thigh will be a start.

My company is handling this party and I want to help, but Kaylee wants this to be her big event, so when she meets with clients, she can point to this fundraiser as proof of her abilities. I've been in charge of big events, so I deferred to her. Besides, my family will be there, and I can spend time with them tonight. If something goes wrong, I'll be there to step in and help.

The doorbell rings, alerting me that Lucas is here. He's on my guest list, so the doorman doesn't need to call up. I pick up my silver purse, check my makeup in the mirror, draw a deep breath, and walk through my apartment to let him in.

I open the door to see a dozen roses before I see Lucas standing behind them, the vase in his hands. "Oh, they're beautiful! Come in!" I don't want him to have to stand outside with the heavy flowers and glass holder any longer than he has to.

Once inside, I guide him to the half-circle console in the entryway, and he sets the bouquet down.

"Thank you! They're lovely."

"And to think I didn't know you'd be wearing a matching dress." He looks me over with a hungry gaze, his eyes deepening to a moss-colored green. "Forget the flowers, you look stunning," he says, taking my hand in his.

"Thank you. You look handsome in that tux." Actually, handsome doesn't do him justice. He looked hot in the jacket and white-collared shirt he wore to the club, but tonight? Debonair is more like it.

He lifts my hand and presses a kiss to the top. "I wouldn't want to mess that perfect red lipstick," he tells me. "At least not yet."

The sweep of his lips, his gruff voice, and the promise of later almost cause me to combust on the spot, and a small moan escapes from the back of my throat.

"Jesus," he mutters. "We should get going before I strip you out of that dress and we don't make it to the gala."

My panties are now wet. "Can we skip it?" I hear the need in my voice. It matches the way my body is vibrating with desire.

"Don't tempt me. But both of our families will be there, and we'll have no excuse for not showing up as planned."

I treat him to an exaggerated pout. "Fine." But it isn't. Because once we arrive at the hotel, where the fundraiser is being held, we can't flirt, hold hands, kiss, or do any of the things that now feel natural when I'm with Lucas.

A little while later, we enter the elaborately decorated ballroom side by side. I catch sight of my family but before walking over to where they're gathered, I deliberately brush my fingers over Lucas's hand. It's our official parting for the night, and as I watch him head in the opposite direction, where his parents are seated, I feel the loss.

"Rainey!" I turn at the sound of my mother's voice.

"Hi, Mom!" I give her a hug.

"You look beautiful. You know, that dress reminds me of…"

"The night we met." My father joins her and gives me a kiss on the cheek. "Hi, honey."

"Hi, Dad. Having fun?" I ask.

He stares at me. "Do I ever have fun at these events?"

Mom rolls her eyes and nudges him with her elbow. "He's having a wonderful time."

"You met at the Meridian Hotel, right? The one your father owned?" I ask my dad.

He nods. "Your cousin, Asher, bought it and it's closed for renovations right now." Then Dad says, "I see someone I need to speak to, I'll be back."

He strides off and I laugh. "That's Dad for you."

Mom grins. "You should have seen his mood the first time we met. He'd come to celebrate his father's birthday, so you can only imagine."

I nod. I've never met my grandfather, at least not

that I can recall, and from the stories my family tells, I'm better off. I have my mom's stepmother, Melissa, and my dad's mom, Grandma Emma, and her second husband, Michael. Not to mention all my aunts and uncles and, of course, my brothers. We're an overwhelming bunch.

"Hey, sis! Mom." Hudson walks over and hugs us both.

"There's my charming brother. I haven't talked to you in too long."

Although I did hear from the twins after the rock through the window incident, I reassured them Dad had a company redo the security at the office and had a talk with my doormen. I knew better than to argue. A Dare man would do whatever he wanted.

Kind of like Lucas. At the thought of him, I glance across the room to see him laughing at something his father said. As if he senses my stare, he turns and meets my gaze. He treats me to a wink, and I feel better for having connected with him.

Turning back to Hudson before anyone notices I'm ogling someone across the room, I ask, "Anyway, what's going on?"

He grins, his smile reminding me of Mom's and mine. "Work has me buried," he admits. "Miles too. But I should have been in touch more."

"Did I hear my name?" Miles walks over.

Both my brothers look handsome in their tuxedos, but where Hudson is light in his personality, Miles is serious, more like Dad. But they both have Dad's jet-black hair and the Dare indigo eyes.

"Hi!" I step up and give Miles a hug. "I was just complaining to Hudson that I haven't heard from him lately. Same for you!"

He winces. "I'm sure my reason is the same as his. Work. But that's no excuse."

"It's okay. I'm just giving you both a hard time. I've been crazy busy too and could have reached out."

"I'm going to check out the auction items. Let my kids catch up." Mom touches my shoulder. "I'll see you at the table."

"Bye, Mom," Hudson and Miles say at the same time.

A waitress walks by and I accept a glass of champagne from her tray, taking a sip of the bubbly liquid.

"How's the Thunder anniversary party planning going?" Hudson asks.

I tell him about the huge glitch but make him promise not to repeat the issue to our dad. "I've ordered replacement banners, and the swag for the party should be arriving soon. All the items for the museum exhibit were delivered and are being set up. I'll be going to check those out soon." With Lucas, though I don't mention that to the twins. "So basically, things are almost moving along as planned," I say.

"And nothing more from whoever threw the brick?" Miles asks, his brooding expression growing more thunderous as he asks the question.

I shake my head. Since they don't equate the two issues, I don't mention it, either. "So let's talk about more interesting things!" I say, eager to change the subject.

We catch up some more before splitting up to network. This might be a fundraiser to raise money for a good cause but at the end of the day, with all the important people here, be here and be seen is the motto of the night. There are many guests here who might be impressed enough to hire our company, so I need to start chatting.

I spend twenty minutes or so stopping at various cliques I recognize and accepting the accolades for the gorgeous décor and anything else that impressed them thus far. I'm sure to mention Kaylee's name as I circulate so she gets the well-deserved recognition.

A hand rests on my shoulder and I turn, surprised to see Lucas standing beside me. Apparently, I've worked my way around the entire room.

"Hello, beautiful," he says in a low voice.

I can't help but smile up at him. "Hi, yourself."

I stare into his green eyes, our gazes connecting. And lingering.

"Lucas, who is this pretty girl?" a woman I recognize as his mother asks.

It's been years since I've seen her, back when Jack lived home and still needed rides to see his friends and vice versa.

"Mom, this is Rainey Dare. Rainey, my mother, Jacinda Carras."

Her eyes open wide. "Rainey, it's been years. You've grown up! I didn't recognize you. I'm so sorry."

"It's fine. It's good to see you." I smile at the pretty woman with a blonde bob framing her made-up face. I want to hug her for taking Lucas in when he needed parents so badly, but I know that's inappropriate. And weird. But I think it just the same.

"Actually, I've heard so much about you!" she says.

"You have?"

"Mom!" Lucas's cheeks turn red on his clean-shaven face.

I think it's adorable.

"Lucas tells me he's helping you with the Miami Thunder anniversary and you're doing a wonderful job."

I meet his gaze, surprised he's mentioned me. "Oh. Well, thank you both. I'm doing the best I can. It's been… stressful but things happen during planning. Lucas has been a huge help."

"Of course he has." She looks to him, her smile wide. The pride in her expression is obvious and makes me smile.

"Jacinda?" a male voice calls.

She shrugs and sends me an apologetic glance, her eyes soft. "I have to be going. My husband is calling. It's been wonderful seeing you, Rainey."

Before I can reply, she leans close and whispers, "You make a beautiful couple," before turning and gliding away in her beautiful, royal blue gown.

My cheeks are burning as I look up at Lucas. "What was that about?"

"Just Mom being Mom." He takes my elbow and guides me through the ballroom and past the string quartet playing in the corner.

"Where are we going?" I ask, confused.

"Somewhere alone so I can kiss you," he says in a gruff voice.

Immediately, my body responds, my nipples hard peaks, and as much as I want to go with him, I also want to throttle him because I'm wearing a silk dress.

The last thing I need is someone noticing! "Lucas!" I hiss. "We're going home together. We need to wait," I say regretfully.

"Just one—"

"Rainey!" a female voice calls out.

I turn to see Blaire Reynolds waving to me, and

Lucas is forced to stop and release my elbow.

"Blaire. How are you?" I force out. I knew she would be here but was hoping to avoid her. Her M.O. is to fawn all over me while hating me behind my back.

She treats me to a fake smile. "You and Kaylee have done a wonderful job here." She sweeps her arm around, and I take in the greenery woven into draperies on the ceiling and the tall centerpieces with white lilies inside.

"Thank you so much. But we were just stepping out for a moment." I tug on Lucas's tuxedo jacket, now willing to sneak out with him.

"Aren't you going to introduce me to your *friend?*"

I sigh. "Lucas Carras, this is Blaire Reynolds. She owns Sun Coast Events. Blaire, Lucas," I say, tipping my head toward him.

"It's so nice to meet you." She stares as if unable to take her eyes off him.

I clear my throat. "Really, we need to be going."

"Did you know that Rainey and I went to high school together?" she asks.

"No, I didn't know that," Lucas says. "It's a pleasure to meet you, too."

She tucks a strand of blonde hair behind her ear. "I'm not surprised she hasn't mentioned me. When we *met*," she says, using finger-quotes, "Rainey said she didn't remember me from high school."

"We had a large graduating class," I murmur. The conversation was uncomfortable the first time we'd had it, and it never got any easier considering she mentions it every time we run into each other.

"We had a different group of friends," Blaire says. "You know how it is. Cliques and all. But we ended up in the same profession. Friendly competitors!" she all but chirps.

"This is interesting, but we do need to—"

"Get going. Yes. Well, take care. I'm sure I'll see you around, Rainey. Maybe I'll have gotten the job next time." She waves her fingers at us and walks away.

"What was that about?" Lucas asks.

"A competitor. In many ways." I pause, then say, "She's an odd one. But good at what she does. We're just… better. And she has a hard time handling it. But I'm used to her." I shrug.

"Now can we sneak out?"

I'm about to give in when the lights flash, the signal that it's time for the sit-down meal. "I'll be missed if I don't take my seat." I squeeze his hand and release it. "We'll make up for it later. I promise."

I sit through the speeches, barely taste my meal, and talk to my family, not even registering what they say because all I want to do is be with Lucas. Miles slips out of his seat, and my mother takes his place.

"Someone can't take their eyes off the table next to us. And since it's the Carras family and their friends, I think it's Lucas you're staring at."

God, Mom is always so intuitive. "You can't tell Jack!"

"Tell him what?" Her eyes crinkle in confusion. "That you have a thing for Lucas?"

"I don't have a thing for him."

"Rainey Noelle, you can't lie worth a damn. You never could." Mom laughs.

"I'm only Rainey Noelle when I'm in trouble," I mutter.

"You're not in trouble. I've just caught you in a lie. Okay, so maybe you don't have a *thing* for Lucas. Maybe you're already head over heels."

I cough on my own saliva at her words. "I'm not—"

"Lie." She picks up a clean fork, takes a bite of the chocolate cake at my brother's seat, and pops it into her mouth.

"Fine," I hiss under my breath. "But you can't tell anyone. Especially not Dad or Jack. Or the twins."

She places her hand over mine on the table. "If you want to talk about why it's a secret, I'm here to listen."

I swallow hard. "I appreciate that, Mom. But you

wouldn't understand."

"Try me. I went through a lot before actually admitting my feelings for your father. You'd be surprised what I understand." She turns in her seat so she's facing me.

Looking at her, I'm struck by the resemblance, from our long, wavy, chocolate brown hair to the freckles on our nose despite us both wearing foundation. I smile, then get back to thinking and talking about Lucas.

"It's just that professionally, I'm trying to rebuild the business from the Atwater fiasco and Lucas is helping me do that. I don't want to be seen as unprofessional in any way."

Mom tips her head to the side. "And you think being with Lucas is unprofessional?"

I nod. "While we're working together, yes. But there's also Jack. They're best friends and business partners. Jack never let any of his friends near me that way. He threatened anyone who tried. I can't come between them. And I don't want to mess up their partnership."

It's my turn to grab a fork and dig into the cake, then shove it into my mouth so I can savor the taste. I swallow and lift a glass, taking a sip of water before putting it back down. "And there's that old bro code saying: you don't date your best friend's sister."

Mom shakes her head. "Since when do you care what your brothers think? If Jack is upset, he'll have to get over it."

I take another sip of water. "And Dad?" I ask.

"What does Dad have to do with anything?" she asks. Now her crinkled eyes give her an even more confused expression.

I glance across the table to where my father is deep in conversation with Hudson. "When we were younger, I remember you and Dad warning Jack to stay away from Lucas." I keep my voice low. I don't want anyone to overhear.

"When he first came to live with his foster family and he was getting in trouble, yes. But obviously he's changed. He's your brother's partner now. The past is the past." She shakes her head and sighs. "I see you've given this a lot of thought." She reaches out and cups my face in her hand. "My sweet girl. Always the overthinker."

"If you overthink, you can't make mistakes." I shrug because those words defined how I tried to behave my entire life.

Mom treats me to a soft smile. "If you overthink, you can miss out on the most wonderful things." She taps my nose. "Give that some thought."

"Any chance I can steal my chair back?" Miles asks.

Mom nods. She turns to me. "Remember what we talked about, Rainey. And give that your *long thought* treatment."

Smiling, she rises from her seat and my brother lowers himself into the now empty chair.

"Everything okay?" he asks.

"Just fine," I lie. "Just fine."

CHAPTER SEVENTEEN

Lucas

*F*UCK. I'M SO glad tonight is over. I'm not the kind of guy who likes to schmooze with others, shake hands, and make nice. While doing all of those things, I had my eye on Rainey. That red dress with the slit up her thigh, the silk and the way it draped her curves, had my mouth watering and my dick hard.

Now, as we meet up at the entrance, all I want is to get her alone. The valet brings my car around and we climb in. Because we weren't together all night, no one would think anything of us leaving at the same time. We're just two friends, one driving the other home.

I wait until we're alone and pulling away from the hotel before asking, "You're place or mine?" I flip on my blinker and make a right. "Mine's closer," I tell her. Not by much but at this point, seconds matter.

"Yours," she says, placing her hand on my thigh. High up on my thigh. I grip the steering wheel harder. "Do not move your hand or we won't make it home," I manage to tell her, desire a live wire inside me.

The drive home seems to take forever despite it

being a mere twenty-minute trip. We have company in the elevator, another couple, so we stand side by side in silence, waiting for them to walk out on the twentieth floor. Seconds later, we reach mine on the twenty-second.

No sooner do we step into the apartment than I shut the door and sweep her into my arms. I can't make it past the entry and family room, need pulsing through my body. I stop by the sofa and lower her to her feet.

"What are you doing?" she asks.

"Taking you right here." I shrug off my jacket and lay it on the couch, then unbutton my pants. I kick off my shoes next.

Her eyes widen but she catches on and begins to pull her dress up from the bottom until she reveals a nude thong. It's so skimpy she might as well not be wearing anything at all, and my dick begins to throb harder.

She slides the gown up and over her head, tossing it onto my jacket on the sofa. Now she's just wearing a bra that holds up her perfect, full breasts, that sexy scrap of underwear, and a strappy silver pair of high-heeled sandals. As I watch, my fingers still on the zipper of my slacks, she hooks her fingers into the sides of her panties and pulls them down over her hips and from there, they fall to the floor.

She reaches for her bra next and as I've seen her do before, she unhooks the garment and lets it drop to the floor too. Her heavy breasts call to me and I want to suck one of those dusky nipples into my mouth, so I shake my head and get with the program.

I slide the zipper down and over my thick, aching cock and remove my pants along with my boxer briefs, kicking both aside. I pull off my socks and sit down on the sofa. My dick stands tall and as she takes a few steps toward me, I grab my erection and grasp it hard, pumping my hand up and down my shaft. All it serves to do is arouse me even more.

"Come sit," I encourage her, and pat my lap.

Her eyes darken and she does as I ask, straddling my thighs as she sits down, her pussy rubbing against my cock.

"I want to taste you," I tell her.

"Then why am I on your lap?" Her lips curve into a smile.

"Because I want to taste your tits." I cup one breast in my hand and lean down, pulling her nipple into my mouth and sucking hard, teasing the rigid tip with first my tongue, then grazing it with my teeth.

"Oh God." She wraps one hand around the back of my head, pulling me close, forcing herself deeper into my mouth. I lick the tip then suckle hard. Soon, she's circling her hips, leaning forward and grinding her clit against my rigid erection.

I release her nipple with a pop, then grasp her hips and hold on. "Take what you need, beautiful," I say through clenched teeth. Because I'm barely holding on, having no desire to come before I'm buried deep inside her.

She's arching her back and rubbing her pussy against me, her breaths coming in shorter and shorter pants. Reaching up with one hand, I take her other nipple between my fingers and pinch it tight before I release it.

A shuddering moan escapes her and she begins to tremble. "I'm coming," she says, and I lean back to watch her as her orgasm takes over. Her lips are parted in a small O, her eyes closed, and if I had to describe how she looks, it's someone experiencing pure bliss. She's completely lost in the sensation. Knowing that I'm the one she's getting off on is a high I've never had before. My pulse pounds and my cock is wet from her arousal.

She's a limp mess by the time she's done, and I'm so hot for her I feel ready to explode. I brush her hair off her face and she smiles up at me, a satisfied grin on her pretty face.

"Ready for more?" I ask her.

"I'll give it my best try," she says on a light laugh. Then, she rises up and grasps my erection in her hand, positioning herself over me and sliding down easily.

I groan, the utter rightness of being cushioned inside her impossible to deny. I shift my weight and raise my hips. Her tight walls squeeze me in her heat. We move in unison, her riding me as I keep up with her rhythm. She's rising up and dropping back down, her breasts bouncing with every bit of movement. I shift so I meet her each time, and I feel the beginning of my climax traveling through me.

My balls draw up but I need her to come first. Before I can slide my hand to reach her clit, she clasps my cock hard, cries out, and her release washes over her. I let myself go, slamming my hips upward once, twice… and then I'm coming, releasing so hard I nearly black out, but I'm aware enough to know she comes, another climax taking over before we're both a sated, sweaty mess.

She climbs off me and I feel the cool air on my cock. Slowly, we rise to our feet. "Want to share a shower?" I ask.

She nods. "But all I'm capable of is a shower," she warns me. "My legs feel like noodles and I'm exhausted.

I raise one hand. "No funny business. Promise."

"Don't you mean sexy business?" she asks.

I grasp her hand and lead her to the bathroom. I pull out two fluffy towels and drape them over the counter. My mother bought them for me when I moved in because I'd have picked up one for myself and not worried about anything else. I turn on the hot water and we step under the spray.

Keeping my promise and my hands off her isn't easy, but I manage, watching as she uses my soap, massages shampoo into her scalp, and rinses. Luckily, I have conditioner even if I don't use it—again, thanks to Mom, who helped stock this place. We wash ourselves, ignoring the sexual tension and my renewed erection, thanks to the fact that she's naked, gorgeous, and she's going to smell like me, which is a huge turn-on.

Once we're clean and dry, I walk naked into the bedroom and collect a pair of boxer briefs for me and an old T-shirt of mine for Rainey. I leave her to get the dampness out of her hair with the small blow-dryer I have, and a few minutes later, she walks into my room. She's petite in height and blessed with gorgeous curves, and my shirt hangs to her knees.

At the sight of her in my clothing, a possessive growl rises from my throat. "Get in here." I flip over the comforter on her side of the bed.

She presses a knee to the mattress and climbs in beside me. Unable to help myself, I hook an arm around her and pull her to me for a long kiss. "No funny stuff," I say against her lips. "I just needed to taste you again."

She sighs and curls into me, her still slightly damp hair on my shoulder. The silence is peaceful and I close my eyes, too aware of how right Rainey feels here, in my apartment, snuggled against me in my bed. What we have isn't just sex. It's a connection I've never experienced before. One I don't want to lose.

I tangle my hands in her hair and she lets out a soft little moan. As I play with the long strands, I wonder if I have to… lose her. She doesn't want us to be a public couple now and I can respect that. I have respected that. But she thinks things will end after we're finished with her Miami Thunder anniversary project. Again, why does it have to end? Jack is the biggest obstacle, but would he really begrudge me finding love even if it is with his sister?

Love.

I love Rainey and I can't tell her. It's the last thing she would want to hear right now. But later? Once Jack comes home? I want to take the risk and tell him I have feelings for his sister.

As she lies in my arms, I decide that's exactly what I'm going to do. I fought my way to being a good guy.

I'm going to fight for her.

CHAPTER EIGHTEEN

Rainey

I WAKE UP surrounded by heat. My body is a furnace, and I open my eyes to find I'm pressed against Lucas's hard chest, his arms wrapped around me. I breathe in his spicy masculine scent and suddenly, I don't mind the heat.

"Morning," he says.

I break our connection and push myself off him so I can meet his gaze. "Morning."

"Sleep well?" he asks me.

Better than I normally do alone. But I don't say that. "Very. How about you?"

"Amazingly well."

He stretches and I take in his bare chest, the stretch of his muscles, and the morning scruff on his face. He's so handsome, especially this relaxed and with his guard down.

"And the gala? Did you have fun?" he asks.

I don't need to think. "Kaylee did an amazing job. It will set her up as someone to be respected in the business."

"Like the Thunder will do for you."

I smile. "That's the hope. I had a nice time but…"

"What?"

"I wished we weren't forced to pretend we're just friends or acquaintances," I admit, placing a hand on his warm chest.

He nods. "I felt the same way."

I wonder if he'll say anything more about us, but he remains silent. "Umm… it was good seeing your parents again after all these years. I like your mom."

"She's great and I definitely got the feeling she likes you."

I think back to her comment about us and my curiosity grows. "Can I ask you something?"

Reaching out, he curls a strand of my hair around one finger, something I'm learning he likes to do. "Anything."

I bite down on the inside of my cheek, then ask, "What did your mother mean by saying we make a beautiful couple? Does she know we're together?"

"She has mom instincts and a need to meddle. I think that was her way of telling me you're good for me." He tugs on the lock of hair he's twirled. "And she's right."

"I have another question." This one he might not want to answer, but since talking to his mom last night, it's been niggling at me.

"Go ahead."

I pick up the hand that's not in my hair, and thread my fingers through his. "Will you tell me what happened to your parents?"

He lets out a low groan, then is quiet for so long I think he's not going to tell me.

He meets my gaze. "Well, I already mentioned my mother was a drug addict and my father was a drunk, frequenting the neighborhood bar. And he never tried to stop her using."

"You did tell me that." I squeeze his hand in mine, wanting him to know I'm here for him.

He unwraps my hair, and rolls to his back, placing one arm beneath his head, staring up at the ceiling. "One night, my father came home from work and Mom had been beaten up by her dealer. He wanted the money she owed him and… she didn't have it. The guy tried to get it from my father, but he'd spent all his cash on alcohol. Her dealer shot them both."

I gasp, but he doesn't tear his gaze from the ceiling. "Luckily for me, the neighbors heard the gunshot and called the police, or I would have been the one to find them."

"Lucas," I say on a shocked breath.

Lost in thought, he continues. "When I arrived home, there were cop cars outside. Apparently, one of the neighbors told them about me, so they waited until

I showed up." He shakes his head. "Of course, I saw the cop cars and panicked, thinking they were after me. I'd been out shoplifting with the guys."

He sounds disgusted with himself, and I brush a hand over his shoulder. It's the only comfort I can offer him.

"They took me to the station. Someone from child protective services came. I was placed in a temporary home before the miracle of Jacinda and Matthew happened. I mean, how many sixteen-year-old troubled kids are placed in a permanent home?"

"A very lucky one." I scoot over, lift myself up, and press a kiss to his warm lips. "I appreciate you sharing that with me. And I'm proud of where you ended up in life."

"Well, I appreciate you listening and seeing the best in me." He shocks me by reaching over and rolling me on top of him. "Now, how about we eat breakfast?"

"I would say yes… except there's something very hard poking at my stomach and I believe we need to take care of that first." A rush of arousal pools between my thighs as his erection makes itself known.

"I like the way you think."

Grinning, I push myself down his body and take care of the *problem*. Later, we share pancakes for breakfast and talk about a variety of lighter things, getting to know each other better. From favorite book genres—romance for me, thrillers for him—to best loved movies, we share the little things in our lives. And though we might not share tastes in the same specific genres, we both like to read, watch movies, and stream on TV.

And that is good enough for me.

CHAPTER NINETEEN

Rainey

I HANG UP the phone with the caterers for the anniversary party, satisfied the menu is set for the evening. I check that off my to-do list and move on to the next item. I've been working all morning, and I'm about ready to take a break.

My phone rings.

I glance at the screen and see it's Lucas. My stomach flips at the sight of his name. After spending a glorious night and day in his bed, I returned to work on Monday and I've been busy ever since. But we've texted during the day, talked after work, and the end result is scary. I'm getting used to my days with Lucas in them.

The only way I can deal with the upcoming end of our relationship, which I'd said was after our work together ended, but more likely would be when Jack returns from his last stop in Charleston, is by telling myself what I feel for Lucas is attraction.

Desire.

Admiration.

Not love.

I'm lying to myself and I know it.

Drawing a deep breath, I answer the call. "Hi, Lucas."

"Hi, beautiful." My heart squeezes at the endearment and my body grows soft at his gruff voice.

"What can I do for you, Mr. Carras?" I ask, keeping things light.

"Adam called. It's time to visit the museum and see the exhibit in person."

I wish I can say I put my ex out of my mind, but he's on the to-do list for the anniversary season events. "I'm surprised he didn't call me himself."

There is silence before Lucas says, "I might have told him to stay the fuck away from you the last time I was there."

I open, then close my mouth before finally bursting out in laughter. "Oh God. I know I should be mad you weren't completely professional with him but…"

"He said some things about you I didn't like. Nobody talks shit about you around me."

My heart skips a beat at the alpha-possessive tone in his voice. Lucas doesn't apologize for what he said to Adam and I don't blame him. I like the fact that he stood up for me. Isn't that why I'd sent him to begin with?

"I wasn't going to give you a hard time. I'm happy

you put him in his place."

"Good, because even if you were upset, he deserved the warning," Lucas says.

I nod even though he can't see me. "Yes, he did. I'm just shocked he listened to you."

"Despite Adam's bluster, I'm pretty sure I intimidated him," Lucas says.

I have no doubt he's right. "And I would have loved to see that. So, what's the plan?"

"Can I pick you up and we'll go this afternoon?" he asks.

"Yes. The sooner we get it over with, the better." And then I can deal with anything that goes wrong, but at least the long sessions with Adam will be over.

"Okay. I'll pick you up at two. That work?" Lucas asks.

I glance at my smartwatch. That's thirty minutes from now. "Sounds good," I tell him.

"I'm looking forward to seeing you. It's been too long." His voice drops to a husky whisper.

"It's been three days," I tell him, though I feel the same way. I've missed the easy rapport we have when we're together. Phone calls and texts just aren't the same.

"Three days too long. See you soon," he says, and we disconnect the call.

Instead of working for the next half hour, I walk

into the office bathroom and fix my makeup.

Not for Adam, but for Lucas.

I return to the office. Kaylee had been on the phone when I made the plans, but she's off now. "I'm going with Lucas to check out the exhibit at the museum."

She glances up from her laptop. "Promise me if that snake, Adam, tries anything, you'll knee him in the balls." She grins at the thought.

Laughing, I say, "I'm sure Lucas will do it before I get the chance."

She lets out a sigh. "I wish I had a man who'd kick someone in the balls for me," she says wistfully.

I roll my eyes. "You're ridiculous."

She shrugs her shoulder and grins. "But that's why I'm your bestie!"

What can I say? She's right.

It's brutally hot out, so I wait inside for Lucas. Instead of making him get out to come get me, I walk out when I see him pull up in his convertible. Given the heat and humidity, the top isn't down and I open the passenger door before he can climb out his side.

"Hi!" I say, as I slam the door.

"Hi, yourself," he says with his patented charming grin. But it's his eyes, the warm look in them, that he seems to save just for me.

I lean over and he meets me halfway. Our lips lock

and the feel of his kiss after a mere three days is everything I need. I lean back slowly and touch my mouth. "My gloss is gone."

"My girl doesn't need makeup."

Though I blush, it might be the nicest compliment I've ever received. And him calling me his girl? Butterflies take flight in my stomach.

"Ready to deal with the jackass?" he asks.

I laugh. "Ready as I'll ever be."

We drive over to the museum to the sound of Hozier playing on the radio. I'm not worried about seeing Adam because I'm not alone, and if he's smart and wants a feather in his cap by running the Thunder Anniversary Collection, he'll behave. Lucas is my insurance that I won't have a problem.

We enter the museum and walk together to the room where the display is located. The sign we'd ordered looks perfect above the doorway, and I step inside to find the history of the Thunder surrounding me. Team memorabilia that I'd had on my list but am now seeing in person brings a proud lump to my throat. Throwback helmets, uniforms, jerseys, and balls, signed and unsigned. Mint silver coins, autographed photographs, trophies, Funko Pops of star players, and so much more.

"I did a fabulous job, right?"

I turn to face Adam and feel Lucas's hand against

my back. "I think the items I had sent over speak for themselves," I tell him in my most annoyed voice.

"Isn't that just like her? Taking credit when I did all the work." Adam slides his hands into his front pockets.

I grind my back teeth. "I'm going to check out each case and we can get going," I tell Lucas. The sooner I view everything in the room, the faster I can get away from Adam.

He's on his best behavior so far, which is never saying much, but I'll take it.

Although the memorabilia are about the team, I can't help but feel it's my family's legacy. My great-uncle Paul owned the team first and because he has no children, he groomed my dad for the position of president. Uncle Paul now travels the world with his partner, Lou, and checks in often. And, as it turns out, he has a family, the Prescotts, who are also well-known in sports.

"Ahem. Are you paying attention?" Adam asks, interrupting my thoughts about my interesting family tree. "I was saying that I strategically placed things to encourage people to circle the room counterclockwise and exit through that door." He points across the room to another exit door.

"That should work," I say.

Since Lucas hasn't left my side, I'm aware when his

phone buzzes in his pants pocket. We'd shut our ringers before we entered the museum. He pulls the cell out, looks at the screen, and groans. "I need to take this."

"Go ahead. I'm fine."

He shoots Adam a pointed look. "I'll be right over there and watching you." As he accepts the call, he tips his head and strides over to the far corner of the room.

"I still can't believe you need your Neanderthal boyfriend to come see me," Adam grouses.

I raise my eyebrows. "I'm here to see the exhibit, not you," I remind him.

"Why are you always such a bitch? You weren't like this when we were together."

"Because we weren't together all that long and you didn't show your true colors until I turned down your proposal. Which, by the way, is the best thing I've ever done."

At the reminder, his face turns a mottled shade of red. "You cunt." He raises a hand as if to slap me, and before I can take him out by the balls, as Kaylee suggested, Lucas grasps Adam's wrist and yanks it behind his back.

"You're finished," Lucas says through clenched teeth. He tightens his hold on Adam's wrist.

"Ouch. Let me fucking go." He attempts to shift

out of Lucas's grasp.

Lucas holds on for a few more, what must be painful, seconds and releases him.

"Let's go, Rainey." He wraps an arm around me and we walk out of the exhibit room.

I swallow hard.

"That son of a bitch. If we weren't in a museum, I'd have beat him to a pulp." I look up at him to see a vein throbbing in his temple.

I glance around and see a man seated behind the information desk. "Come with me," I tell Lucas.

We reach the older gentleman. "How can I help you?" he asks.

"I'd like to see the director," I tell him.

After reporting Adam to his boss for inappropriate behavior, we walk out of the museum, and I feel one hundred pounds lighter.

"I am finished with him." I wipe my hands together as if ridding myself of Adam Roberts for good.

CHAPTER TWENTY

Rainey

I LOOK ACROSS the room at Kaylee.

She looks back and shakes her head, then shrugs.

I run my fingers through my hair and let out a scream of frustration. "How can this be happening *again?*"

We're supposed to be putting together gift bags with the swag and merch I'd ordered for the anniversary party. Instead, I have tissue paper everywhere in the back, empty bags with the Thunder logo, and nothing to put inside them. None of the ordered items arrived at the beginning of the week the way they were supposed to. I waited another few days and they still haven't shown up.

I draw a deep breath and take control. "I'll call the Thunder PR office and ask where their merch is," I say.

"And I'll call the retailers we ordered the glasses and other swag from and ask when they sent everything out." Kaylee picks up her phone and I do the same.

We discover the boxes were shipped and their tracking number says they've arrived. Except they haven't.

"Ashlynn?" I call out. "Can you come in here?"

She walks in, looking tired, bags beneath her eyes. I hadn't seen her when she came in and I'm worried about her.

"What's up?" she asks.

"I know Kaylee and I have been in and out while working the last few days. Did you sign for any deliveries and forget to tell us?" I ask.

She shakes her head. "No. I always check them off based on what we're expecting on the computer. You can see everything I logged in."

I nod. "I assumed that was the case but we're missing shipments, so I needed to ask."

"Sorry," she says in a soft voice.

"Are you okay? I don't mean this badly, but you look exhausted. Is there anything we can do?" I gesture between myself and Kaylee.

"My grandfather is sick and I was at the hospital late the last couple of days."

I glance at my partner and as if reading my mind, Kaylee nods.

I turn to Ashlynn. "There's nothing we need you to do today. With the deliveries missing, we're at a standstill. Why don't you go home and get some sleep?" I offer.

She shakes her head. "I couldn't."

"Of course you can." I step over and put a hand on her shoulder. "I know it's hard when someone in your family is sick. I'm offering you time to catch up. Take it."

"Okay." She glances at me, then Kaylee. "Thank you both. You're amazing bosses." Head down, she walks back to the front of the office.

"Poor kid. She looked like she was about to fall over," Kaylee says. "I'm glad she's going home. Now… back to our issue." As I think about how to fix yet another blow to the anniversary celebration, I begin to pace the floor between our desks.

"So, forgetting the swag for now, the merch from the Thunder is an issue. The guy I spoke to on the phone said they don't have enough on hand to send more." His exact words were, they don't have enough *current* merchandise. But that doesn't mean they don't have older items from years past. Like vintage merch. "Wait! I have an idea!"

I stride to my desk, grab my phone, and call my aunt Olivia, an executive in the Thunder front office. After I explain my predicament and pitch my idea, she tells me to come by and she'll give me the keys to the storage room where old merch is kept. I thank her and promise to be right over.

"Aunt Olivia saves the day!" I say, knowing Kaylee overheard my side of the conversation.

She smiles and waves. "Then get going!"

I leave Kaylee to work on swag she can get on short notice and head over to the stadium where Aunt Olivia said to meet her.

On the drive, I ponder ideas and themes that will explain the older merchandise I fill the bags with. I'm assuming I can find T-shirts with old logos, bobble-heads, and Funko Pops, even if not everyone gets the same player, team hats, jerseys, and other items, all with old logos, I should be set.

Celebrating history.

That will be my new party theme.

After I arrive, I rush to the storage room, not stopping to see any of my relatives first. In the room, I hit pay dirt. Everything I hoped for and more is stored there. I pull my hair into a bun atop my head, sit on the floor, spend an hour taking notes so I know what I have available to use, and put sticky notes on the boxes and items I want to take.

My next call is to Lucas. I ask him to bring his SUV over to haul the items I've found back to my office, and he agrees. I give him directions to the front offices and where to go once inside. By the time I'm finished typing ideas into lists on my phone, Lucas arrives.

He walks through the door, and it shuts behind him. Instead of his usual long-sleeved shirt and slacks, he's wearing a pair of black track pants and a T-shirt cut at the sleeves. His biceps bulge on his arms and he's just so good-looking, I could stare at him all day.

"Hey!" he says.

"Hi. I hope I didn't interrupt your workout?"

"Nah. I was just stepping out of the shower at the gym. I threw this on and here I am. My truck's outside."

"Well, I really appreciate the help. I put sticky notes on what we need to load into the car. I just can't risk shipping things and them going missing again." At the thought of all that lost merchandise from the team and items I paid for, again from the budget I'm working within, nausea hits.

He walks toward me, his brow furrowed. "Again?"

I sigh and hold up a hand. He pulls me to my feet as I tell him about the issue with the missing shipments and my idea to come here and see what I could find to replace things.

He shakes his head and his gaze narrows. "We thought the banners could be sabotage, but now I'm sure someone is deliberately trying to undermine you."

I press my palms against my eyes and groan. "I've been so consumed with fixing everything that broke I barely had time to think about that. Who would do this to me?"

He shakes his head because he doesn't know who's behind this any more than I do. Stepping closer, he pulls me into his arms, and I feel safer being close to him. "I stopped being afraid once things quieted down after the brick throwing."

"I know. I gave Adam some thought after our trip to the museum. Especially after reporting him. I'm sure they let him go."

"I'd think so. We were pretty specific with what he's said and they won't want him around patrons after that." I tip my head back and meet Lucas's gaze. "But all this started before that day." With the post-card.

"Doesn't mean it's not him. Maybe we need to hire a PI to look into things."

I nod and rise to my toes, wrapping my arms around his neck. "Why are you so smart?"

He laughs. "Flattery will get you everywhere." He leans down and his lips cover mine. Mint explodes in my mouth as we kiss but it's *his* need that makes me feel good. Cared for. I slip my tongue between his lips and—

"What the hell?"

At the sound of my brother Hudson's voice, I push away from Lucas.

"Rainey? *Lucas?* Really? What are you two doing

making out like teenagers in our storage room?"

"I—"

"How long has this been going on?" Hudson asks, shock giving way to what seems to be anger, and I panic.

"It's not—I mean, we haven't discussed what it is." My cheeks are hot and I know they must be red with embarrassment. Someone in my family catching us is my worst nightmare. It's going to get back to Jack and he's going to lose his mind. Me and his best friend. His business partner. It will feel like such a betrayal.

"It doesn't matter what *this* is," Lucas says. "It's *something*, and it's between us."

Hudson looks from Lucas to me and shakes his head. "Jack is coming home tomorrow."

My eyes open wide. I had no idea, but Lucas doesn't look surprised. I assume he planned on telling me after we got through my work issues, but it doesn't matter. Jack is going to be hurt that his best friend did anything with his sister. He and Hudson are close, he won't keep this to himself.

"Oh God. I need air." I brush past both men and rush from the room, ignoring Lucas calling my name.

CHAPTER TWENTY-ONE

Lucas

"**S**HIT." I RUN a hand through my hair, torn between rushing after Rainey and dealing with her pissed-off brother.

"That's one way of putting it," Hudson says, a scowl on his face.

Of all the ways for my relationship with Rainey to come out, getting caught lip-locked in the Thunder storage room never crossed my mind. Hudson stands glaring at me, and I meet his gaze head-on. The twins are twenty-six to my twenty-nine but they're solid, muscular, and protective as hell over Rainey. The same as her father and Jack.

"Look, I know you're pissed and I know better than to tell you not to mention this to Jack. Just know it's not a fling. Not for me." Those are the only words I'm giving him. "Now, I need to go find your sister. And, by the way, I'll be back to pick up the items she wants for the party."

I push past her brother and rush out the door, going back the way I came, knowing I have to find

Rainey. Stepping into the muggy sunshine, I see her getting into her car, and I jog to catch her before she drives away.

"Rainey!" I call as I stop by her side of the vehicle and knock on the window.

She pulls it down instead of opening the door and getting out of the vehicle. Her eyes are red-rimmed, her skin is pale, and it breaks my heart to see her so upset.

"I promise you, we'll work this out," I say, and I'm determined to do just that.

She shakes her head. "I thought we could tell Jack about us together. On our time. Now things are going to blow up before the anniversary party and with everything else going wrong, it's the last thing I have time to deal with."

"Get out of the car. I want to talk to you." I grab the handle and with a sigh, she clicks the unlock button. I open her door and extend a hand. She places hers in mine and I pull her from the vehicle, directly into my arms.

I wrap my hands around her waist and keep her against me. "Did I just hear you say you thought we could tell Jack about us together? As in, you weren't going to walk away when the anniversary events are over?"

She blows out a long breath. "I didn't think about

it, exactly. I just knew it was going to be hard, if not impossible to… separate when things were over. And I knew Jack's return would speed things up. I just didn't know he'd be home so fast."

I have to laugh. "He's been gone for a while. He had to return sometime."

"I know." She presses her palms to her eyes. "But it's too soon."

I grasp her wrists and lower her hands so I can see her face. "Maybe it's exactly the right time. I can deal with your brother, Rainey. I can even face your parents."

She wrinkles her nose, confusion on her face. "What do my parents have to do with anything?"

"We need to talk, but I don't want to do it here. Are you in the mood to hit up the food truck again?" Hopefully we can find a bench to sit on while I explain my concerns about her family, what they really think of me and how it could impact us.

"But what about the boxes from the storage room? I wasn't thinking straight when I was going to drive away without them," she says.

"How about this: you said the ones you want have sticky notes on them, right?"

She nods.

"I'll load them up and bring them to your office. Then we can go eat and talk."

She throws her arms around my neck and hugs me tight. "Thank you!"

I know how much her family means to her, and I have no idea what she'll do if her father and brothers really don't approve of our relationship. But she deserves to know what's on my mind and think things through before she has to face them.

A couple of hours later, the merchandise is loaded in the back room of her office. I put the last box down and turn to see her lining the empty goodie bags on the long tables set up along the wall by the new window in the back.

As if sensing my gaze, she turns. "Lucas?"

"Yes?"

"I was thinking. Maybe we can order in food and fill goodie bags while we talk? Kaylee texted me that her sister was in a minor car accident but she's at the hospital with her. And I have a feeling she'll need to watch her niece, at least for tonight. I need to do these bags alone so…"

I walk over and brush my knuckles over her cheek. "You already know, if you need me, I'm here. I just need to let Tristan know I'll be in late tonight."

"Thank you. Really."

I wink at her, then pull my phone from my pocket and text my partner.

Rainey and I order lunch. The pizza won't be as

good as the food truck, but I don't care what we eat as long as we're together. Then we get to work. It's a lot, filling the bags, folding and rolling T-shirts before putting them inside, among other things. And when the food arrives, we agree to take a break.

I wait until we finish eating and clean up the garbage before I ask her to sit down again at the small table we set up for our late lunch. So late it's almost dinnertime.

"Okay, I think you've stalled long enough. What's on your mind?" she asks.

She's right. This isn't a conversation I'm comfortable having, but it's necessary. "So, here's the thing. Even when we get Jack on board with our relationship—"

"*When?* You're so sure we can get Jack to accept us?" she asks.

I nod. "I am. I can handle him." He wants someone who will take care of his sister, and that's me. He'll get over the shock and anger. In time. "It's your father I'm worried about. I know how much you love your parents and don't want to disappoint them."

She takes a sip of her soda from one of the cans we'd gotten with our order. "Why would me being with you upset them?" She props her chin on her hands. "I really don't understand."

It's better to lay things out for her, starting at the

beginning. "What did your father think of me when Jack and I became friends? What did he tell you about me?"

She meets my gaze, her cheeks flushed. "If we're being honest, he wasn't happy when he found out about your past. Or the things you got in trouble for when you first came to live with the Carrases."

I nod. Despite her confirming what I already know, and even despite understanding that Ian Dare had every reason not to want his kids around me back then, it hurts to hear the truth.

"I'm not so sure his feelings have changed." When she opens her mouth, I hold up a hand. "At least not when it comes to his precious daughter." And the last thing I want to do is come between Rainey and her father.

Her brothers? I'm not lying when I tell her I believe I can handle them.

Ian Dare? I'm not so sure.

She rises from her seat and sets her hands on her hips, looking at me with a disappointed look of her own. "Lucas Carras, you are not the same man as the boy you were."

I let out a chuckle because—"You sound like my mom."

She treats me to a beautiful and wide smile. "That's quite the compliment since she strikes me as a very smart woman. She said we make a beautiful couple, after all."

I manage a smile. "I appreciate your optimism but—"

"How about you let me handle my parents and we'll deal with Jack together?"

I take her hand. "I like that idea." Us being together is the goal.

"I'm not dismissing your concerns, though I think they belong in the past. But when we agreed to a fling, I wanted to keep things a secret because I was afraid it would look unprofessional to be with someone I'm working with."

"I remember." I also recall not liking it, but I'm not going to mention that now.

She raises her shoulders in a shrug. "I was wrong. I was so hung up on what happened to me in the past with Gregory Attwater and my career that I restricted myself and tried to make everything perfect."

"Oh yeah?" I ask her.

She rises and walks around the table, coming up beside me and sitting on my lap. "Yeah. It's being with you that's perfect," she murmurs.

"I couldn't agree more," I say, as she seals her lips to mine.

I respond, loving the taste and feel of her, but my mind isn't on the kiss. As optimistic as she seems, I'm more concerned about what her family will say. Because I won't be satisfied until I have her brother's one free shot at hitting me behind us, and her father's blessing.

CHAPTER TWENTY-TWO

Rainey

I WAKE UP the next morning after a fitful night's sleep. Once I finished with the goodie bags, Lucas followed me to my apartment to make sure I arrived safely before he headed back home. He's such a gentleman but so hung up on the mistakes of his past, he doesn't see himself the way the rest of the world does. But I'm determined to show him he's wrong. Especially about my father. I don't miss the irony, though. While I'm worried about Jack's reaction, he's concerned about my dad's.

Though I have calls to make to assure myself all the vendors will show up for the anniversary party, I need to take care of something for Lucas first. I call ahead to see where I can find my father. He isn't going into the office today, so here I am on my parents' front porch.

I ring the bell and Dad answers the door. Instead of his usual suit and tie, he's in a pair of khakis and a short-sleeved polo shirt. "Hi, princess. Come in."

I step into the house and he shuts the door behind

me, then gives me a hug. "Come into the kitchen. Mom's out doing some grocery shopping. You know how she loves to do normal chores."

I laugh. "Yes, Mom doesn't let you spoil her in basic ways."

While Dad can afford a chef and a housekeeper, Mom insists on doing most of those things herself. She didn't grow up wealthy like he did and she wanted us kids to know how to care for ourselves. What we decide to do as adults is up to us. I'm more like Mom. I cook, clean—though I have a cleaning crew come in often—and grocery shop. I'm determined to be a capable grown-up. Of course, Dad spoils her in other ways. A private jet, an island retreat, and more jewelry than she wants or can wear.

He's set the standard by which I judge men, and it just so happens Lucas meets that high standard, which is why I'm here.

"Coffee?" he asks.

I nod. "I'll take care of it."

I walk over to the Nespresso machine and make us each a steaming cup of coffee. From the fridge, I take out the vanilla almond creamer for me and the plain one for Dad.

Once we're set, I sit beside him on a high barstool around the center island.

"What's up, kiddo?"

I'm transported back to when I was a kid with the nickname that preceded princess. I take a sip of hot coffee and try to convince myself I feel the jolt of caffeine flowing through my veins. In reality, I'm sure it takes much longer than that.

I clear my throat and meet his gaze. "I'm seeing Lucas Carras and before you say anything, I need you to hear me out. He thinks you still have issues with him because of his childhood and the trouble he got into. And if you do, you're wrong. He's a good man. He's been there for me through everything going on with the party issues. He makes sure I get home safely. He hears me. Like, really listens to what I have to say and doesn't forget. When Adam got nasty with me, Lucas stepped up. He threatened him and protected me. All his issues are in the past and—"

"You love him."

I stare at my father, wide-eyed. "I do," I whisper.

"Can I speak now?" he asks with a grin.

I nod. "Sorry for the rambling. Go ahead."

He lifts his coffee mug and takes a drink before putting it down and meeting my gaze. "I know about you and Lucas. Hudson called."

I roll my eyes. "Of course he did."

"He loves you, Rainey. He's just looking out for you," Dad says.

"Yeah. He loves me so much I'm sure his first call

was to Jack. To get him all worked up and pissed off at Lucas." I curl my hands around the granite counter's edge.

Dad shakes his head. "You had to know this relationship would come with… complications. But not from me."

"No?"

"As far as I'm concerned, Lucas grew up. Changed. Became a decent man. Everyone has a past. It's what you do going forward that matters."

I let out a relieved breath. "I knew it," I say out loud.

Dad rises to his feet. "You mentioned some other things. Like party issues? And Adam *threatening you?*" His voice rises with that last one.

Oh damn. I rambled on so much about Lucas, I revealed things I meant to keep to myself. I put my hand on his arm. "Dad, it's all being handled." Not that I think mere words will calm him down.

"By you. And you want to be independent and take care of things yourself," he says, repeating words I've used with him before.

"Not just by me. By me and Lucas. Like I said, he's handled Adam and you know he had the broken window replaced for me. And the other stuff involves some missing merchandise and swag, but I'm making things work. It's going to be a great party. I promise."

He runs a hand through his hair and groans. "Is that what you think I'm worried about?"

"Yes?"

"No! I'm worried about you!" he yells, just as the door sensor beeps and my mother walks through the side door by the kitchen, grocery bags in hand.

"What is going on? I can hear you yelling outside!"

Dad paces the floor and turns to Mom. "My daughter just let it slip that she's having issues with that jackass Adam again, and with missing merchandise and orders. On top of the brick through her window that was never resolved. And she thinks I'm worried about the party. I'm worried about her!"

Mom places the grocery bags on the counter and walks over to him, wrapping an arm around his shoulders. "Ian, take a deep breath and calm down."

To the surprise of no one who knows the effect my mother has on her husband, he listens. He draws a deep breath and lets it out. There's a reason we call her the *Ian Whisperer.*

"Good." She looks at me and winks. "I'm sure Rainey has things under control. Right, Rainey?"

I nod. "Right. I told him Lucas and I are handling things." If Dad knows about Lucas, I have no doubt he told Mom, who pretended she didn't already know.

"See? They're handling things," Mom says. She glances at the table and narrows her gaze. "You're drinking coffee, Ian? Is it regular or decaf?"

"I made it and it's regular. Why would Dad need decaf?" I ask, suddenly worried about my father.

Dad shakes his head. "Riley, we agreed to keep that quiet!"

Mom winces. "Sorry. I slipped. Your father has high blood pressure, but he's on medication and he's fine. But he's calmer without the caffeine."

"Dad! We need to know these things. Do my brothers know?" I ask.

"No!" my parents say at the same time.

Well, that's good. At least I'm not the only one in the dark. "Dad, no more caffeine for you." I pick up his mug, walk to the sink, and dump out the contents, then rinse it with water.

Dad looks at me, a small smile on his face, then turns and gives Mom the same half grin. "You two. My head is spinning. And, Riley, you didn't react to the news about Adam, which means… you knew."

"I knew," she admits. "But this is why we didn't tell you. You're upset and we didn't want you to…"

"Get all protective," I say. "I knew you'd be angry that I'm dealing with him, but the museum exhibit for the team is an amazing idea, so it was the right thing to do. It's not my fault Adam is the curator. Besides, Lucas was the go-between. Everything's fine. I might have gotten Adam fired for being a disrespectful, rude jerk, but other than that, it's all good." I spread my hands out in front of me. "See? Handled."

Dad turns to my mother. "Why did we have so many children?"

"Because you like sex," Mom says without flinching.

I cringe. "That's it. I'm leaving!" My parents have always been overly affectionate and that hasn't changed. Mom is in Dad's arms right now. "I don't want to hear about my parents having sex!" I step over to them, and Mom separates from Dad so I can give him a hug. "Thank you for what you said about Lucas," I tell him.

"I never say what I don't mean. I love you, princess. I only want the best for you. As for you and Lucas, I'm fine, but good luck with Jack."

Dad winks at me and I let out an *ARGH* sound, throwing my hands up in the air. "Bye, Mom! Bye, Dad! I love you both!" I say, rinsing out my own coffee mug before picking up my bag and walking out the kitchen door my mom entered through.

I pause, my hand on the doorknob. "Do you happen to know if Jack is back, and if so, where is he?"

"He called when he landed. And if I had to guess, he went straight to see Lucas."

I groan and rush out of their house and over to my car. Next stop? Lucas's apartment.

CHAPTER TWENTY-THREE

Lucas

I'M STANDING IN my bathroom with a towel wrapped around my waist when my phone buzzes. I glance down at the text from the front desk.

Jack Dare is here to see me.

"Fuck." I message back to let him in. Then, I run a towel over my hair, change into a pair of track pants, and walk out to meet him.

I can't say I'm surprised by the visit. Ever since Hudson caught Rainey and me kissing in the storage room, I've been expecting a text, a call, or for him to drop by after he arrived back in Miami. Apparently, he had an early flight.

A loud knock sounds on my door, and I open it to let him in.

Jack looks me over from my bare feet, up past my pants, to my exposed chest, and scowls. "Where is she?" Jack storms past me into my apartment.

"She's not here." No way will I play dumb with my best friend. "Sit down and we'll talk."

Next thing I know, he swings, his fist connecting

with my jaw. "That's for breaking bro code," he mutters.

"And that's the only free one you get." I rub my throbbing jaw. "Now sit the fuck down and let's discuss things like civilized people."

Jack's frown deepens. "My sister? Really? And you're making out with her in a storage closet like she's not worth—"

"Do not finish that sentence," I warn him. Without another word, I turn my back to him and head into the great room off the kitchen. I take a seat in a club chair and wait for him to do the same. Hopefully across the room from me.

From my teenage years running with a rough crowed, I know how to take a hit… and give one as well, but that's not what I want with my friend and Rainey's brother.

Jack sits down in the matching chair, so there's a large cocktail table between us. He rubs his hand over the back of his neck as he shakes his head. "She's my sister and she deserves respect."

I narrow my gaze. "What makes you think she won't get that from me?" Does he really think I'm dumb enough to fuck up our friendship and our business by treating Rainey like shit?

Jack catches my gaze and stares. "Really? Mr. I Don't Date and They All Know the Score? Or do you give them more than a night or two, then dump them when they get too close? Is that what you're doing with Rainey?"

"That insinuation is offensive, but I can see why you made the assumption." I draw a deep breath and let it out. Lucas is well aware of my past. What he doesn't know is how it's affected me. I'm not one to bare my soul. Rainey's gotten more of me than anyone before her; looks like I'm going to have to give Jack *something*.

I lean forward, elbows on my thighs, my hands dangling between my legs. "I admit to how I've treated women in the past. No, I didn't let anyone get close. Did you ever wonder why?" Before Jack can answer, I go on. "When your own parents don't give a shit if you come home for dinner, eat, or even show up at night to go to sleep, you get used to being treated like an afterthought." I swallow over the lump now in my throat. "I dumped those women before they could do the same to me. And let's not forget, they all knew my lack of intentions going into things."

He winces, the friend in him feeling bad for me, something I neither want nor need. "I never knew any of that."

My lips lift in a wry grin. "We're men. Do we ever talk to each other about feelings?"

He lets out a laugh that gives me hope we'll work

our way past this.

"And my sister?" he asks. "Does she know the score, too?" Jack rubs a hand over his face and groans. "Because I've got to tell you, the idea of you treating her like all those others doesn't sit well with me. Even if I understand your reasons."

I take the time to gather my thoughts before answering. The sun streams through the extra-large windows and I pick up a remote and click a button. Slowly, the window treatments begin to close and kill the glare.

"Your sister is different," I finally tell him. "She has been from the beginning. We both tried to fight the attraction and when we couldn't do it anymore, we agreed to end things when the Thunder party was over. And to keep things quiet so we didn't hurt you. She's been worried sick about what you'll do when you find out." And I doubt she'll be happy when she sees the bruise he no doubt left on my jaw.

Jack shakes his head. "I'm not hurt. I'm worried about my sister getting her heart broken," he mutters.

"That's not going to happen."

He narrows his gaze. "Because it's just a fling?" he asks in disgust.

"Because I love her!" I shout, then rise to my feet and begin to pace. "I don't think Rainey or I ever truly believed we could walk away when the event was finished. We've gotten too close. She's a special woman."

I glance at my friend who's merely watching me carefully. Listening.

"I admire Rainey's work ethic. I appreciate how she cares about her friends, family, and employees. I love her smile and her laugh. I like how she'll eat a huge sandwich in front of me and not blink an eye. No salad for her. And I adore the freckles on the bridge of her nose."

"That's enough." Jack holds up a hand, an uncomfortable look crossing his face. "I get it." He pushes himself up and stands, then walks over to where I'm leaning against the bookshelves lining the wall. "Those intimacy issues you had?"

"I can't say they're gone completely. But being with Rainey has taught me to trust. And if you think back, when was the last time I was with another woman?"

Jack remains silent.

"Right. It's been a long while. I've been working on myself, whether you knew it or not. I have been since I let Matthew and Jacinda in. Since I trusted them."

"And Rainey knows all this?" Jack asks.

I nod. "No secrets." I meet his gaze. "I'm committed," I assure him, and extend my hand.

Jack doesn't pause before shaking it. "But cliché or not, you hurt her and next time I won't just punch you, I'll break your jaw."

And no matter how much I can protect myself, I know he means it.

Good thing I have no intention of doing anything to Rainey but protecting her and making her happy.

Once he's calm, we talk about his trip and the various locations he scouted, and I learn he'd been in Charleston the longest.

"I—"

A knock sounds on my door, which means it's someone on my automatically "allow up" list. I doubt it's my parents, so that only means… Rainey.

"Hang on, Jack. I'll be right back." I hope to talk to her before she goes off on her brother once she sees my jaw. I know it's red and will turn black and blue eventually. But it's no big deal.

"Sure." He rises to his feet and walks over to the large window.

Once I'm sure he's occupied, I turn and head to the door. I open it and I'm right. It's Rainey. "Hi!"

"Hi." She meets my gaze and her eyes open wide. "What happened?" She gently trails her fingers over my jaw.

"It's nothing. Just two friends coming to an understanding."

"Where is he?" She strides past me, a woman on a mission.

"Rainey, wait." I shut the door and follow her into the family room, her long hair gliding against her back as she walks. "Let's talk about this first," I say, but she's not paying attention.

"Jack!" she calls out.

Her brother turns from his place at the window. "Rainey."

"What the hell do you think you're doing? How could you hit him?" She shoves his shoulder with one hand. "You don't get a say in who I'm with."

Jack sets his jaw. "He's my friend and you're my sister. I have every right to look out for you."

"If he's your friend, then you know he's a good guy! Why would you hit him?"

"Rainey, I told you. It's two friends coming to an understanding. We did and now it's over."

Jack steps forward. "Almost over. I need to talk to you." He grasps her hand. "We'll be right back," he says, and tugs lightly, leading her toward the den for some privacy.

"Do not give her a hard time," I warn my friend as he disappears down the hall with the woman I love.

CHAPTER TWENTY-FOUR

Rainey

I TOOK ONE look at Lucas's bruised jaw and I wanted to throttle my brother. I didn't appreciate being pulled into another room for a talk I didn't see the point in having.

I've spent the last I don't know how many weeks worried about what my brother will think of my feelings and relationship with Lucas, but now that he knows? And reacted irrationally—no matter what Lucas thinks—I'm past the point of caring.

"I can't believe you hit him," I say, glaring at my brother.

"And I can't believe you slept with him!" Jack replies.

I draw in a deep breath and let it out. "It's more than that. We're more than that, and I am sure Lucas already told you as much."

Jack shoves his hands into the front pocket of his slacks. "He did."

I nod, satisfied Lucas and I are on the same page when facing my sibling. "Look, I've been worried about what you'd say about me and Lucas since the beginning. I don't want to hurt you, and I don't want to come between you as friends or partners. But as much as I want you to be happy for me and support us, if you don't, I'm not walking away from him." Tears fill my eyes at both possibilities. Losing Jack because he refuses to accept our relationship and losing Lucas. I only have control over one of those things, and I'm taking it.

I hold my breath and wait for Jack to speak.

He pulls one hand from his pocket and runs it through his hair. "From the time I was a teenager, I warned all my friends to stay away from you. I didn't care that we were younger, I knew some day we'd reach the point where age didn't matter. Dad taught us to be protective of you, and I was. I still am."

"But Lucas is your best friend! And he's two years older than me."

"And I know his past," he says.

"So do I." Once again, I'm feeling emotional and a lump rises to my throat. "He's changed."

Jack nods, his lips pulled into a firm line. "But I also know his history with women."

I admit to myself that that's not something we've discussed in depth, but I do know he hasn't been with another woman in a long time. "Talk to him about that because it has nothing to do with me. We're different than whatever either of us had in the past."

I want to tell Jack I love Lucas, but I haven't said the words to him yet. And he hasn't told me. My brother doesn't get them first.

I narrow my gaze. "So, you hit him?"

"I hit him before we talked," Jack mutters. "And he deserved it. Just ask him."

I roll my eyes. "Men." It's my turn to mutter.

He sighs and walks over, then grasps my arms and meets my gaze. "I know how Lucas feels about you. It's just going to take me time to get used to the idea, that's all."

He sounds pained, like I should feel sorry for *him*. "Like I told you, we did consider your feelings. You weren't supposed to find out the way you did. But, Jack, we're not waiting for you to come around. I need you to deal with us as a couple and accept it. Quickly. Because that's not going to change."

"I love you and I just want what's best for you."

I nod. "I know. And what's best for me is Lucas." I rise to my tiptoes and kiss his cheek. "And, Jack? I love you, too."

We return to the great room where Lucas is staring out the window. At the sound of our footsteps, he turns to face us, his gaze landing on me. "Everything okay?"

I look to Jack. "Is it?"

He nods. "Everything is fine. As long as he treats you well."

I slip my hand in Lucas's bigger one, signaling to Jack that we're a team.

My brother doesn't stay long. His plane had just landed this morning, and he'd come straight to Lucas's to confront him. He wanted to go home and shower. They agreed to meet at the club later so he, Tristan, and Lucas could discuss his findings about each city.

Once he leaves, I relax, my shoulders dropping in relief. "It's done."

Lucas nods. "It's done."

Reaching up, I slide my fingers across his jaw. "I'm sorry."

"I'd take a hit for you any day," he says with his charming grin. "Ask me why."

I crinkle my nose, confused, but I do it anyway. "Why would you take a hit for me?"

He takes my hands in his. "Because I love you, Rainey Dare. This might not be the most romantic setting or way of telling you, but it's true." Lifting my hands, he presses a kiss on my knuckles.

Warmth fills me along with a sense of all being right, finding my guy, security, someone who loves me for me and not my last name.

Grinning, I say, "Well, it's a good thing you do. Because I love you, Lucas Carras. And I told my brother he'd better get used to us because I'm not letting you go."

He cups my face in his hands and lowers his mouth to mine. I expect the kiss to be hard and fast. Instead, it's soft and meaningful. He's not reacting with desire, though that always exists between us, he's reaching for my emotions and revealing his.

He takes his time, delving deep, his tongue sweeping back and forth inside. My stomach flips and my body tingles. I love him, and I'm experiencing what that means for the first time.

Breaking the kiss, he slides his hand against mine and leads me to his bedroom. I remove my high heels and suddenly feel smaller beside him. It's not often that happens, not with my thicker curves. But he seems to appreciate them, a low growl coming from his throat.

His gaze never leaving mine, he undoes the buttons on the back of my sundress, lowers my shoulder straps, and the garment falls to the floor. Before he can rip my panties, I pull them down and step out of them. He immediately reaches around my back and unhooks my bra. Once it joins my other clothes on the floor, I'm naked before him.

All he's wearing is a pair of black track pants, which he easily removes, and I discover he's commando beneath them. I lick my lips at the sight of his cock standing erect, a drop of precum on the tip.

I begin to drop to my knees, but he stops me, hands on my arms. "No, sweetheart. This isn't about me. It's about us."

He lifts me by the waist and places me on the bed. I scoot backward, knowing I'll need the support of the pillows behind me. Desire thrums through my body, my nipples hard peaks, wetness dripping from my sex, and emotional need deep in my belly. But it's my heart that's pulsing in my chest, every beat meant for him.

I lay back and he comes over me, bracing his hands on either side of my head. His cock lays against my sex and he rubs his hard erection over my clit until my arousal begins to grow. The more he moves, the wetter I become, and the more I need him to fill me.

"I need you inside me." The words sound like a plea and they are. I part my thighs wider. "Please, Lucas."

"My pleasure, beautiful." He shifts until his cock is at my entrance and seats himself just inside me.

I close my eyes and whimper at the tease, lifting my hips, pulling him deeper inside me but not enough.

"Look at me," he says, and as I set my gaze on his, he slowly glides inside me, shifting his hips, filling me up, and making sure I feel his thickness until we're fully joined.

When he begins to move, once again it's not hard

and fast, it's with reverence, letting me know how much I mean to him. And if I have any doubt, all I need to do is look into those green orbs to know he's right there with me. Feeling every emotion that's overwhelming me, just as it is him.

He glides in and out, beginning to pick up the pace, his deep stare never breaking. With each thrust, my need grows until he shifts his hips and he takes me harder. It doesn't take long for the familiar tingling to begin. Three more consecutive drives inside me and my release takes over. I'm overcome with emotion, my climax a glorious, intense thing that's filled with wonder.

And love.

CHAPTER TWENTY-FIVE

Rainey

I PULL UP to my office and because it's so early, I find a spot out front. Grabbing my tote with all my notes, laptop, and the usual heavy items I tossed in, I walk to the front entrance. Before I can unlock the door, a shadow appears behind me, and I spin around to face whoever it is.

"Adam!" I all but shriek. "Don't sneak up on me like that!"

To my surprise, he takes a step back, holding up both hands. "I just want to talk."

Narrowing my gaze, I say, "So talk." No way am I letting him into the office where I'd be alone with him. I hang the tote bag over one shoulder, fold my arms across my chest, and wait.

He wipes a bead of sweat off his forehead but obviously realizes he's not getting into my air-conditioned office because he starts speaking immediately. "I was fired."

"Good." And not a surprise, I think, as I wait for the explosion of his temper, hoping Kaylee comes in early today, too.

"You reported me, I assume? My supervisor didn't say who complained, just that it was enough for her to know I'm a liability and not an asset."

I narrow my gaze and curl my fingers around my keys, knowing I have nothing on me to use for defense. Then again, he's not angry, sarcastic, or mean. Not yet. "Why are you so calm?"

He runs a hand over his face. "I fucked up."

"Which time?" I ask him. He narrows his gaze and I hold up one hand. "Sorry. Go on." I shouldn't be antagonizing him while he seems civil.

"I've been an arrogant ass. When you said no to my proposal, I snapped. I thought we belonged together—"

"It had been six months, and I'd given you no indication I was ready for that."

He nods. "I realize that now."

"Adam, I have to ask. What's with the nice guy act?"

I try to think if I've seen this side of him when we started dating, and I honestly can't remember. I never considered us to be serious, although when I date someone, I'm exclusive. I'm not the type of woman to jump from man to man.

"When my supervisor let me go, she told me I had talent in my field and that she'd give me a good reference, but she couldn't have me working for the museum anymore." He pauses, sliding his hands into his pants pockets. "I was pissed. Went to the nearest bar and drank until I couldn't stand."

I wince.

"I don't remember calling my father for a ride, but apparently, I did. When I woke up in my childhood bed, I looked in the mirror, and I didn't like what I saw." He hesitates, then says, "Neither did my family. And they sat me down to tell me about it."

"That couldn't have been easy."

He shakes his head. "I took a ride along A1A and stopped to look at the ocean. And I realized I could go on the way I have been, thinking I was God's gift to women—though frankly, only my mother believes that—or I could wake up, get my act together, and try to be a decent man." He pauses. "I'm going with trying to being the good guy for once."

My mouth parts in surprise. "I don't know what to say." Or whether to believe him.

"I don't blame you. But I came to apologize. Explain. And to tell you I took a job at a museum in California. I think distance is good right now."

There's so much to digest from this conversation that I don't know where to begin. I could start with, is he really leaving? Am I finished dealing with him in any way?

I meet his gaze. "I wish you well, Adam." It's all I can manage.

"Thank you. Same to you, Rainey. Be well."

I watch as he walks down the street, and I hope that's the last I see of my ex.

CHAPTER TWENTY-SIX

Rainey

A FEW WEEKS later, the day of the Thunder anniversary party arrives, and I thought I'd be a nervous bundle of energy. Instead, I'm calm and determined. I'd slept at Lucas's last night and we took two cars to the club this morning. He lets us inside where I wait for Kaylee, Ashlynn, the two assistants we use for parties, and the electrician and handyman who will help with setup. The florist is due to show up in a few hours before the party begins. It's a well-choreographed affair, one we've done before, but never with so much at stake, at least for me.

The girls are setting up the goodie bags on a large table. I'm still excited about the vintage merch we've put inside each. Kaylee and I watch the handyman set up the banners, and I do my best not to get upset we don't have the tapestries because they would have been stunning. But when the banners are set around the room with the spotlight over each, I take it in and I can breathe. They stand out just as I'd hoped and everyone who walks in will notice them.

"Looking good!" Kaylee puts her arm around my shoulders. "I have to say, glitches and all, this place is perfection."

"It is, isn't it? Once the florist arrives, it'll look even better." I envision the tables with bouquets with team colors on each and can't help but smile.

As we admire our handiwork, Ashlynn walks up to us. "The florist is here. He's going to bring things in from the back. The caterers also just showed up. The kitchen has their own doors so they won't conflict with the flowers being brought in."

I nod. "That's good." I walk to the back delivery entrance and greet the florist.

"Rainey!" Adrian says, wrapping me up in a big hug. "Always good to see you."

"Same here! We're ready for you, so go do your beautiful thing!" I gesture toward the inside of the club and leave him to it.

As I pass the hallway, a hand reaches out and grasps my wrist, pulling me back against a hard chest. I never panic. I recognize Lucas's familiar, spicy scent and relax into him.

"The club looks fantastic," he says, his deep voice in my ear.

I grin. "I'm pretty pleased. The florist is here and so are the caterers. I'm going to check the kitchen next."

"Want company?" he asks, kissing the side of my neck. A tremor ripples through my body at his touch.

"Always," I murmur.

We walk side by side to the industrial kitchen in time to see the food laid out on the counters. I glance down and freeze. "What is this?" I ask of what appears to be vegetarian appetizers. My heart begins to pound double time.

"Are you okay?" Lucas asks.

I shake my head as the caterer, a woman named Sherri who I've never worked with before, but who'd been excited about offering a variety of selections for a football anniversary party, walks over to me.

"What's wrong?" she asks, as she lifts the wrapping off the top of one of the trays.

My mouth is dry so I gesture to the food containers. "They're all vegetables," I manage to say.

She nods. "Yes. That's what you said you wanted when you called to make changes to the menu."

I stiffen and glance at Lucas. "I assure you I did not call. This is a party with football players attending. More men than women. They're going to want meat. The glamour burgers we discussed. Tacos handed out. Not cauliflower and broccoli!" I say, my voice rising.

Lucas places a calming hand on my back, but it doesn't work. I'm shaking with panic.

The caterer's eyes open wide. "I don't understand. I spoke to you."

"It wasn't me! Why didn't you send me a new confirmation and menu list?" I ask.

"I did send one." She walks to the counter and begins looking through her tote. "Here." She pulls out the contract with an amendment, then a separate menu, and hands me both. "You signed them."

My head is spinning as I accept the papers and look through them until I reach the signature page. I compare the original contract with my signature to the amendment and though at a glance, it's close enough to mine, there are subtle differences. Besides, I know I didn't receive or sign it.

"It's not my signature." I hand her back the paperwork.

"But—"

I blow out a long breath. "I'm not saying you could know. But something's very wrong." I glance at Lucas. "Can we talk?"

He nods. The blood rushing to my head, I follow him out of the kitchen, through the club, and down the hall to his office.

"What's going on?" he asks.

I tug at my ponytail in frustration. "Whoever's sabotaging me is someone close. They work with me. Have access to my files and my computer."

He nods.

"Which leaves only Kaylee and Ashlynn. And I am

telling you, it's not Kaylee." Even the thought makes me nauseous.

Lucas raises an eyebrow. "Ashlynn?" he asks.

"I don't want to think so, but who else can it be?" I shake my head, my thoughts spinning. Why? Why would someone I've been so good to try and destroy me and my business? I don't understand.

"What do you want to do?" Lucas asks.

I pull my phone from my jeans pocket and text Kaylee, giving her a brief rundown and asking her where Ashlynn is.

"Ashlynn is blowing up balloons. I'll talk to her in a few minutes, but what am I going to do about the food? I can't feed a bunch of men the rabbit food in the kitchen!"

"Breathe," he says, brushing my ponytail to one side and massaging the muscles in my neck. "I'm going to make a few phone calls and see what I can do for catering. Meanwhile, get Kaylee so you can both confront Ashlynn."

"But—"

"Teamwork, remember?" He kisses the back of my neck. "Now, go."

I'm nervous, but I trust Lucas. If nothing else, I know he'll try his best to fix things. After texting Kaylee again, I step out of the office and meet her at the end of the hallway.

"You're kidding me, right?" she asks.

I shake my head. "Not about the food and not about Ashlynn," I say, lowering my voice. "Unless you can think of anyone else with that kind of private access?"

She lowers her shoulders in disappointment. "No."

I'm feeling the same sadness as my partner. "I know," I say softly. "I trusted her, too."

"She's worked for us for over a year. Why would she undermine us?" Kaylee asks.

"Why don't we find out?"

Kaylee nods and together, we walk over to where our assistant is sitting by a helium machine, blowing up black and gold balloons. Head tipped down, she doesn't notice us.

Ashlynn is young, twenty-two, and she'd been looking for a job for a while when she'd sent us her résumé. During the interview, her exuberance and diligence impressed us. We gave her a shot when she had no experience in party planning and until today, we haven't been disappointed. True, the past few months she'd been more tired and distracted, but everyone goes through rough patches. Now, I have to wonder exactly what is going on with her.

"Ashlynn?" I ask.

She looks up, holding one uninflated balloon. "Hi, guys!"

"Kaylee and I need to talk to you," I say.

She puts the balloon down and rises to her feet. "Sure. Do you need me to work on something else?"

I glance at my partner. "No. But I do need to ask, did you call the caterer and ask her to change the menu for tonight to all vegetarian?" I watch her carefully, wanting to catch any indication she's lying when she replies, except I don't have to.

Ashlynn bursts into tears. "I'm so sorry. I didn't want to do it. Any of it. But she offered me money and with my grandfather so sick, and him not having insurance, I needed the cash for his medication."

My eyes open wide. "Ash, who paid you to sabotage this party?" I ask, my voice hoarse. Even knowing it couldn't be anyone else, I didn't want to believe it was her.

She swipes beneath her eyes, smudging her mascara. "Blaire. She said the more events you took on, the worse she'd look. You succeed at everything you do, and she has to struggle with your leftovers. To be honest, it didn't matter why. It was the money I needed. I hated doing this to you both." She sniffs and finds a tissue in her purse beside her. She's a mess, but I have bigger problems.

"You're telling me she paid you to ruin this party because she's jealous?" Kaylee asks. Her voice is loud and shrill, and I don't blame her.

"She wanted to make Rainey look incompetent. It's more about you than Kaylee," Ashlynn says, looking at me with regret in her eyes.

I don't understand why she'd hate me this much, but that is a question for another day. "Ashlynn, you could have come to us instead of doing as she asked." I'm hurt that she didn't feel she could.

"She gave me a lot of money." The young woman hangs her head, her embarrassment clear.

I shake my head and sigh. A glance at Kaylee and I know she'll agree with what I'm about to do. Do I feel bad for her because her grandfather is sick? That she needs money? Of course. But that doesn't justify her actions.

"You can take your things and go," I say in a firm voice. I trusted her and she not only betrayed that trust, she tried to destroy the business Kaylee and I have been building.

Kaylee nods in agreement.

Without arguing, she rises to her feet. "I'm sorry," she whispers, then turns and walks away.

"She got off easy," Kaylee mutters.

"I know and we can talk about how to proceed later. It's Blaire I really need to worry about." Something tells me she won't stop until I'm out of business and my reputation is in tatters. Something I've meticulously rebuilt since the Attwater fiasco.

Kaylee lets out a frustrated groan. "You're in charge here, so it's your call. What do we do about the food?"

"I still don't know," I say, frustration rising inside me, tears burning in my eyes.

"Rainey!" Lucas's deep masculine voice calls my name.

We both spin toward him, but he's already reached us thanks to his long strides. "Problem solved!"

"How?" It's almost impossible to believe he's found someone able to provide food on such short notice.

Lucas grins. "It pays to have friends. One of the guys from my childhood went into business with his father. They opened a barbeque restaurant, and I convinced them to shut down to customers for the day to make food for your event. What self-respecting player doesn't like wings and ribs? Buffalo, barbeque, garlic parmesan…"

I release the breath I've been holding. "Oh my God, you're amazing!"

"You really are," Kaylee says, a grin on her face.

Looking proud of himself, he holds up one hand. "Wait. There's more. I called around and there's a burger place willing to send burgers. Not just any burgers, either. He does toppings like truffle aioli, fig jam, and blue cheese."

"Lucas!" I rush him and wrap my arms around his neck. "You just saved this party!" I say, pressing a long kiss to his strong, firm lips before releasing him.

Then, I think things through, and my mood grows more serious. "This must cost a fortune! Between the food and covering the cost of them shutting down for the day?" I'll eat the loss. I have to. It's not like the caterer who thinks I called her and changed the menu will refund the money.

Beside me, Kaylee remains silent. She, too, understands the ramifications of what's happened.

Lucas braces his hands on my waist. "It's worth it," he says. "You're worth it."

I open my eyes wide. "You can't mean you're paying for the food?!"

"It's covered," he says, his tone confident.

I look from Kaylee to Lucas, staring and mute. There are no words to describe what I'm feeling. From relief that the party can go on as planned to disbelief Lucas would do such a thing to stubborn refusal to accept his money. But that's a discussion we can have later.

"Thank you! I'm going to talk to the caterer and explain she'll set up at a side table for people who prefer vegetarian options, and have her make room in the kitchen for all the food that's coming."

"I can handle the caterer," Kaylee says. "I'm sure

you have plenty of other things to do." She tips her head toward Lucas.

I blow her a kiss, and mouth, "I owe you," to her.

She grins and rushes off to the kitchen.

I meet Lucas's gaze. I consider myself an independent woman who can handle any crisis. I would have found a solution to the food problem, but the fact that I didn't have to? That someone not part of my company, someone who just cares for me, stepped up and handled it? My heart is so full.

"Thank you. I will pay you back. This is a company expense, but I'm so grateful you figured it all out for me." I hug him once more. "Now, I need to get back to work."

He nods. And as I walk away, I think I hear him say, "Not paying me back, sweetheart."

I shake my head and decide to deal with financial issues later.

CHAPTER TWENTY-SEVEN

Rainey

S UCCESS.

As I glance around at the happy guests, devouring wings, burgers, ribs, and even the vegetarian appetizers, a sense of satisfaction fills me. There are three serving stations. One has wings, another has burgers, and the third has the ribs. Servers are walking around offering the appetizers and the specialty drinks, which Mak is mixing behind the bar. I'd made sure she'd be working as one of the bartenders so her unique drinks are made perfectly.

No one would know there were any glitches in the planning. I'd gone home to change into my outfit for the night and though I'm still working, I look like I'm one of the attendees.

The players are walking around like the royalty they are, taking photographs by their banners and dancing. And my family is here, those who work with the team and even those who don't. Although club music is playing now, I have a surprise for the guests later. My uncle Grey, a rock star who retired to write songs for other musicians, is going to play.

"Rainey Noelle Dare, I could not be prouder of you." My father takes me by the shoulders and presses a kiss to my forehead. "From the day you were born, I knew you were special. Thank you for doing this for the team."

"Thanks, Dad." Happiness fills me. "I can't tell you how thrilled I am. It's all perfect."

"You look beautiful, too. Where's your—"

"Lucas?" I ask. "He's with Jack and Tristan. Before that, he was by my side." I smile up at him. "He's good for me, Dad."

"I see that." He places his hand on my back and leads me toward where my mother is standing with Uncle Alex and Aunt Madison.

After spending time with Mom, I check in with the caterers and restaurant owners. Everything is running smoothly, so I take time to mingle with my cousins. I have a lot of them, and we catch up.

Lucas walks over and I take him in. Wearing his usual black slacks, jacket, and white dress shirt, he's still the sexy club owner I used to wish I could get to know better.

Now I do.

"Hey, beautiful. How are you?" he asks.

"I'm great, thanks to you." He shakes his head and gestures around the room. "All of this is due to you, your talent, and determination."

I grin. "If you say so."

He laughs and suddenly his expression changes. "Isn't that the woman we met at the charity gala? She's your competitor, for lack of a better word."

I look over my shoulder toward the entrance and see Blaire walking into the club. "This event is invitation only," I grit out.

"If one of my people let her in or was bribed, I'll handle it," he assures me.

"More like Ashlynn gave her an invite. She can't get away with what she did."

"Rainey!" Kaylee rushes up to me, speaking in a loud whisper. "It's time for you to introduce the speakers." She slips a microphone into my hand.

"I need ten minutes," I tell her. "Let my father know we're starting a little late." As team owner, he's first up to speak.

Anger fueling me, I storm over to where she's standing with Lucas by my side.

"Easy, tiger," Lucas whispers in my ear, placing a hand on my shoulder. "Remember, you're at your own event. You don't want to cause a scene."

I know how to handle myself, but I appreciate the reminder.

"Blaire. I'd ask what you want, but I already know. You're here to see the damage you inflicted." I sweep an arm, gesturing around the room. "Go ahead. See what a successful party looks like." I'm snarky and I don't care.

She looks around, her astute gaze taking everything in, zeroing in on the nearest food station, her mouth parting in a perfect O. "But… But—"

I grab Blaire's elbow. "We need to talk in private."

She sets her jaw and allows me to lead her to Lucas's office. He starts to follow, but I shake my head. This is between me and this woman who has issues with me I don't understand. While walking, I turn my phone's recorder on, determined to get her admission taped.

I place the phone face down on Lucas's desk. "Tell me why. Why have you been trying to sabotage me ever since I won the bid on the Thunder party?" I ask.

She narrows her gaze. "Because you're a bitch and have been since high school. You don't remember me from then even though you were picked for the trip to France for the cultural exchange program and I wasn't."

What?! She's going back to a high school gripe? "It was chosen by grades. How can that be my fault?" I ask.

"You always come out on top! It's not fair. Every time I go for something, you win!" She's yelling as she speaks, her cheeks turning red.

She's irrational but she keeps talking. "I encouraged Gregory Attwater to complain publicly about anything and everything. Luckily, it wasn't hard since nothing makes the man happy, but you rebuilt after that. It's like you never go away!"

I blink in stunned silence as she continues to incriminate herself.

"Everything good falls in your lap. Then this party. You're a Dare, so of course you got the Thunder party bid!"

Staying calm isn't easy, but I manage. "Blaire, I had a solid presentation. They liked my ideas, that's all. I know for a fact nobody in my family pushed for me to get this job."

She rolls her eyes. "Keep telling yourself that," she mutters loudly.

"And the brick?" I ask, because I need to know.

"I threw it in frustration. And I sabotaged this party, and I'll keep trying to ruin you until my company is the only one people will use. And nobody will ever know what I did because it's your word against mine."

"That's where you're wrong," I tell her, flipping over my phone and pointing to the red screen. "I've been recording you this whole time. From vandalism to stalking, I have your admission of criminal activity. I'm sure the police will love to listen."

Blaire's cheeks are already red. Now, tears form in

her eyes.

The door bursts open and Kaylee rushes in, Lucas and my father close behind. "Rainey? Are you okay?" my best friend asks.

"I wasn't waiting another second," Lucas tells me, his gaze holding mine.

"I'm fine." Shaking, but fine. I didn't realize how much adrenaline the confrontation took until now.

Blaire looks to each person in the room, and I almost feel sorry for how humiliated she must be. Almost.

Without another word, she runs from the room.

My father's jaw is clenched tight. "Go after her," he tells Lucas.

I shake my head. "It's not like there's anything we can do about her actions. I'll turn the information over to the police and let them deal with her."

Despite his hesitation, he agrees.

"Dad? I'm sorry this happened at your party."

He shrugs. "A party will never be more important than you. As far as the guests go, nobody knows a thing."

I smile at him, grateful I have him as my father. It takes a while, but I manage to convince everyone to go back to the main event. Despite wanting to be alone with Lucas, I have an event to run. We all exit the office and return to the party.

Microphone in my hand, I step onto the stage where the speeches will take place. "Can I have everyone's attention?" I ask, and wait until things quiet down. "It's time for the speeches, so I'm going to turn the microphone over to the president of the Miami Thunder, Ian Dare."

My father accepts the microphone, and I slip away from the crowd and find Lucas hovering by the hallway entrance. He snags my hand and leads me back to his office where he shuts and locks the door.

Two steps and I'm where I need to be, in his arms. I soak in his warmth and the strength of his embrace, allowing myself to fall apart for the first time. My body shakes but I hold back tears, knowing I'll need to return to the other room looking professional.

"I can't get over the fact that she hates me so much she'd go to those extreme lengths to destroy me and my business," I say.

He places a hand beneath my chin and tips my head up to face him. "I don't think she dislikes you as much as she does herself. It's sad," he says.

I nod. "A part of me doesn't want to go to the police. I feel sorry for Ashlynn and Blaire obviously has issues."

"My concern is if she's unhinged enough to throw the brick just because you won the bid on this event, what will she do next? Maybe if the police get involved, it'll scare her enough to leave you alone."

I sigh. "That makes sense." And it would make me feel better to know she has something to fear. "But not Ashlynn. She was desperate and I really don't think she wanted to hurt us."

"You have a soft heart," he says, brushing his knuckles over my cheek. "You also have mine."

The words mean everything to me but even more importantly, he backs them up with actions every single day. "You have my heart," I tell him. "And I'll do my best to show you how I feel. To never take what we have for granted."

He kisses me for a brief moment before he lifts his head and his gorgeous green eyes stare into mine. "We have a bright future ahead of us, sweetheart. I promise."

"I'm going to hold you to that," I tell him.

And then his lips come down on mine and he kisses me for real.

EPILOGUE

Lucas

R AINEY SANDWICHED THE Thunder's winning season with another party at Midnight to wrap up the 50th anniversary celebrations. The Super Bowl win is a bonus for the team. I'm proud of all she's accomplished for them this season and how she handled both Blaire and Ashlynn with class and grace. With Blaire's admission and arrest, she ultimately pled guilty and was sentenced to community service, and had to pay a hefty fine. Rainey hasn't seen or heard from her since the night of the party.

Now, Rainey is mingling with her family at a successful final event. Wearing a black minidress with chunky gold jewelry, she sparkles.

"Hey." Jack comes up beside me, two drinks in his hands. He gives me one. "I realize this is six months late in coming, but I was wrong. You're the best guy Rainey could have chosen." He lifts his glass and touches it to mine.

We both take a sip of bourbon. I appreciate his admission. But things between us have been normal and after that day at my house and the one punch, we've been fine. I never blamed him, assuming if I had a sister who fell for a guy with my background, I'd feel the same way.

"How are the building permits coming along in Charleston?" I ask of the place we've agreed to open our second nightclub.

"Slow. But that's city bureaucracy for you." He looks around the party, going quiet.

This has been something he's done often since his return. Going quiet. Getting lost in thought. "Hey, you okay?" I ask, and not for the first time.

He nods.

I don't believe him. Something happened on his scouting trip to the three cities. Something that changed him in subtle ways only a close friend would recognize.

Knowing I'm not going to get any information out of him as I've tried many times, I decide to change the subject. "I'm going to ask your sister to marry me," I tell him.

He jerks toward me, eyes wide. "You think you could have prepared me more? Segued into the conversation or something? Congratulations!"

I laugh. "What makes you sure she'll say yes?" I ask, though I'm confident that she will.

We're all but living together in her apartment. It

wasn't a difficult choice. It was easier for me to move my things into hers than all her clothing, toiletries, and *things* into mine.

"I've never seen two people more in love and in sync than you two, expect maybe my parents," Jack says. "Not that you need it, but you have my blessing."

"Thanks, man. That means a lot."

I'd already asked Ian for his permission to marry his daughter. After a stern glare that would have scared off a lesser man, he'd shaken my hand and told me not to hurt her because if I did, he'd hire someone to shoot me.

I'd said, "Fair enough." And walked out of his home shaking. A little.

I glance at my friend. "We've come a long way with this place."

Jack nods. "We have, and I'm proud of what we've accomplished." He puts a hand on my shoulder. "Well, what are you waiting for? Go ask my sister to shackle herself to you for life."

Chuckling, I place my drink down on the table and head off to do just that.

I scan the room and find Rainey standing alone on a balcony, taking in the party, a smile on her face.

I wind my way through the guests and walk up the stairs to where she's standing. "Hey."

Hearing my voice, she turns toward me. "Hey,

yourself."

I hold out my hand. "Take a walk with me? We won't be long. I'll get you back to the party quickly," I promise.

Smiling, she slips her palm against mine. "I'd follow you anywhere."

The pounding in my chest and the nerves inside me ease at her words. We take the elevator upstairs. Although I'd prefer that we were alone, we're using the outside rooftop area for the party. I find an empty corner, pull her into my arms, and look into her beautiful indigo eyes.

"What is it?" she asks, lifting a hand to touch my cheek. "Is everything okay?"

I nod. "Everything is perfect," I assure her. Then, I know it's time. "We started as wary friends."

"Sexually attracted to each other wary friends."

"Yes." I can't help but smile. "Then you asked if we could hide an affair."

Sadness fills her eyes. "I regret how that made you feel. I didn't want to hide you; I thought we had no choice. I really believed we had to end things eventually."

"I know. But you can't account for feelings and what's meant to be. And I truly believe that's us, Rainey. Meant to be."

I'd pulled the ring out with my free hand on the

way up the stairs. Now, I drop to one knee and pop open the box. My heart thunders so loud in my chest, I swear I can hear the sound in my ears.

She gasps.

I think we've done enough talking, so I keep it short and simple. "I love you, Rainey Dare. Will you marry me?" I show her the round brilliant-cut five-carat ring with diamonds around the band.

"Oh my God! Lucas, yes! Yes."

I slide the ring—which fits thanks to a little sleuthing by Kaylee— onto the ring finger of her left hand.

"It's beautiful," she says, staring at the diamond and the setting.

"A classic style ring for a classic woman," I say, rising to my feet.

She pushes onto her toes and seals her lips over mine. A long, deep kiss with sliding sweeps of her tongue and the soft moans that I love.

After a few minutes, I reluctantly break the kiss. "You wouldn't want to call attention to us by getting naked on the rooftop."

"True." She chuckles, her eyes gleaming with happiness. "You have to promise we'll do just that when we're alone at the club."

I sweep her hair off one shoulder. Leaning in, I press my lips to the sensitive spot behind her ear. "I promise," I say in a whisper. "Anything you want will always be yours."

"And I promise to always make you as happy as you make me."

I slide my hand into hers.

"Let's go reveal the happy news," she says.

I squeeze her fingers. "I asked your father for his permission. Had to keep Ian happy."

"And in charge." She giggles.

I look around at the gathering on the rooftop. "Do you want to wait for the party to end?" I know how hard she's worked to end the season on a high note.

She shakes her head. "Half the people here are family, and I know the guys on the team. Everyone will be happy for us. Besides, do you really think I can hide *this*?" She holds out the gleaming ring. "Or the brilliant smile on my face?"

"In that case…" I bend at the knees and pick her up, holding her in my arms as I stride for the elevator. "Let's announce our engagement."

Thanks for reading! What's next?
Falling for Real: Kaylee and Tristan's novella!
Falling for Love: Jack Dare's story!

Want more of Rainey and Lucas? Get an exclusive **bonus epilogue** by going **HERE!**
https://bookhip.com/ZAJRPXN

If you loved Falling for Trouble, check out **The Kingston Family** series, starting with JUST ONE NIGHT!

Want even more Carly books?

CARLY'S BOOKLIST by Series – visit:
https://www.carlyphillips.com/CPBooklist

Sign up for Carly's Newsletter:
https://www.carlyphillips.com/CPNewsletter

Join Carly Phillips' Readers Lounge on Facebook:
https://www.carlyphillips.com/CarlysCorner

Carly on Facebook:
https://www.carlyphillips.com/CPFanpage

Carly on Instagram:
https://www.carlyphillips.com/CPInstagram

Carly's Booklist

newest series listed first

The Dare to Fall Series
Book 1: Falling for Trouble (Rainey Dare & Lucas Carras)
Book 2: Falling for Real (Kaylee Martin & Tristan Hayes)
Book 3: Falling for Love (Sophie Monroe & Jack Dare)

The Sterling Family
Book 1: Just One More Moment (Remington Sterling & Raven Walsh)
Book 2: Just One More Dare (Dex Kingston & Samantha Dare)
Book 3: Just One More Mistletoe (Max Corbin & Brandy Bloom)
Book 4: Just One More Temptation (Fallon Sterling & Noah Powers)
Book 5: Just One More Affair (Jared Sterling & Charlotte Kendall)
Book 6: Just One More Time (Aiden Sterling & Brooke Snyder)
Book 7: Just One More Date (Leo Watson & Camille Hendricks)

The Dirty Dares

Book 1: Just One Dare (Aurora Kingston &
Nick Dare)

Book 2: Just One Kiss (Jade Dare & Knox Sinclair)

Book 3: Just One Taste (Asher Dare &
Nicolette Bettencourt)

Book 4: Just One Fling (Harrison Dare &
Winter Capwell)

Book 5: Just One Tease (Zach Dare &
Hadley Stevens)

Novella: Just One Summer (Maddox James &
Gabriella Davenport)

The Kingston Family

Book 1: Just One Night (Linc Kingston &
Jordan Greene)

Book 2: Just One Scandal (Chloe Kingston &
Beck Daniels)

Book 3: Just One Chance (Xander Kingston &
Sasha Keaton)

Book 4: Just One Spark (Dash Kingston &
Cassidy Forrester)

Just Another Spark – Short Story (Dash &
Cassidy revisited)

Novella: Just One Wish (Axel Forrester &
Tara Stillman)

Dare Nation

Book 1: Dare to Resist (Austin Prescott & Quinn Stone)

Book 2: Dare to Tempt (Damon Prescott & Evie Wolfe)

Book 3: Dare to Play (Jaxon Prescott & Macy Walker)

Book 4: Dare to Stay (Brandon Prescott & Willow James)

Novella: Dare to Tease (Hudson Northfield & Brianne Prescott)

The Sexy Series

Book 1: More Than Sexy (Jason Dare & Faith Lancaster)

Book 2: Twice As Sexy (Tanner Grayson & Scarlett Davis)

Book 3: Better Than Sexy (Landon Bennett & Vivienne Clark)

Novella: Sexy Love (Shane Warden & Amber Davis)

The Knight Brothers

Book 1: Take Me Again (Sebastian Knight & Ashley Easton)

Novella: Take The Bride (Sierra Knight & Ryder Hammond)

Book 2: Take Me Down (Parker Knight & Emily Stevens)

Book 3: Dare Me Tonight (Ethan Knight & Sienna Dare)

Take Me Now – Short Story (Harper Stevens &
Matt Banks)

The New York Dares
Book 1: Dare to Surrender (Gabe Dare &
Isabelle Masters)
Book 2: Dare to Submit (Decklan Dare &
Amanda Collins)
Book 3: Dare to Seduce (Max Savage & Lucy Dare)

Dare to Love Series
Book 1: Dare to Love (Ian Dare & Riley Taylor)
Book 2: Dare to Desire (Alex Dare & Madison Evans)
Book 3: Dare to Touch (Dylan Rhodes & Olivia Dare)
Book 4: Dare to Hold (Scott Dare & Meg Thompson)
Book 5: Dare to Rock (Avery Dare & Grey Kingston)
Book 6: Dare to Take (Tyler Dare & Ella Shaw)
A Very Dare Christmas – Short Story (Ian &
Riley revisited)

Billionaire Bad Boys
Book 1: Going Down Easy (Kaden Barnes &
Lexie Parker)
Book 2: Going Down Fast (Lucas Monroe &
Maxie Sullivan)
Book 3: Going Down Hard (Derek West &
Cassie Storms)

Book 4: Going In Deep (Julian Dane &
Kendall Parker)
Going Down Again – Short Story (Kade &
Lexie revisited)

Bodyguard Bad Boys
Book 1: Rock Me (Ben Hollander &
Summer Michelle)
Book 2: Tempt Me (Austin Rhodes & Mia Atwood)
Novella: His To Protect (Talia Shaw & Shane Landon)

Serendipity Series
Book 1: Serendipity (Ethan Barron &
Faith Harrington)
Book 2: Kismet (Lissa Gardelli & Trevor Dane)
Book 3: Destiny (Nash Barron & Kelly Moss)
Book 4: Fated (Kate Andrews & Nick Mancini)
Book 5: Karma (Dare Barron & Liza McKnight)

Serendipity's Finest
Book 1: Perfect Fit (Michael Marsden & Cara Hartley)
Book 2: Perfect Fling (Erin Marsden & Cole Sanders)
Book 3: Perfect Together (Sam Marsden &
Nicole Farnsworth)
Book 4: Perfect Strangers (Alexa Collins &
Luke Thompson)

Hot Heroes Series
Book 1: Touch You Now (Halley Ward &
Kane Harmon)
Book 2: Hold You Now (Phoebe Ward &
Jake Nichols)
Book 3: Need You Now (Juliette Collins &
Braden Clark)
Book 4: Want You Now (Andi Harmon &
Kyle Davenport)

The Chandler Brothers
Book 1: The Bachelor (Roman Chandler &
Charlotte Bronson)
Book 2: The Playboy (Rick Chandler &
Kendall Sutton)
Book 3: The Heartbreaker (Chase Chandler &
Sloane Carlisle)

The Lucky Series
Book 1: Lucky Charm (Derek Corwin &
Gabrielle Donovan)
Book 2: Lucky Streak (Mike Corwin & Amber
Rose Brennan)
Book 3: Lucky Break (Jason Corwin &
Lauren Perkins)

Costas Sisters
Book 1: Under the Boardwalk (Ariana Costas &
Quinn Donovan)
Book 2: Summer of Love (Zoe Costas &
Ryan Baldwin)

Ty and Hunter
Book 1: Cross My Heart (Lilly Dumont & Ty Benson)
Book 2: Sealed with a Kiss (Molly Gifford &
Daniel Hunter)

The Hot Zone
Book 1: Hot Stuff (Annabelle Jordan &
Brandon Vaughn)
Book 2: Hot Number (Micki Jordan & Damian Fuller)
Book 3: Hot Item (Sophie Jordan & Riley Nash)
Book 4: Hot Property (Amy Stone & John Roper)

The Simply Series
Book 1: Simply Sinful (Kayla Luck &
Kane McDermott)
Book 2: Simply Scandalous (Catherine Luck &
Logan Montgomery)
Book 3: Simply Sensual (Ben Callahan &
Grace Montgomery)
Book 4: Body Heat (Jake Lowell & Brianne Nelson)
Book 5: Simply Sexy (Rina Lowell & Colin Lyons)

The Most Eligible Bachelor Series
Book 1: Kiss Me if You Can (Sam Cooper &
Lexie Davis)
Book 2: Love Me If You Dare (Rafe Mancuso &
Sara Rios)

Carly Classics
Book 1: The Right Choice (Carly Wexler &
Mike Novak)
Book 2: Perfect Partners (Chelsie Russell &
Griffin Stuart)
Book 3: Unexpected Chances (Dylan North &
Holly Evans)
Book 4: Worthy of Love (Kevin Manning &
Nikki Welles)

About the Author

Carly Phillips is the *NY Times*, *Wall Street Journal*, and *USA Today* bestselling author of over eighty sexy contemporary romances featuring hot men, strong women, and the emotionally compelling stories her readers have come to expect and love. She is happily married to her college sweetheart and lives outside New York City. She is the mother of two adult daughters and a Havanese puppy who stars on her social media and newsletter. Visit her website: www.carly phillips.com.

www.ingramcontent.com/pod-product-compliance
Lightning Source LLC
Chambersburg PA
CBHW071137180726
48291CB00007B/2225